rock *and a* hard place

Also by
A n g i e   S t a n t o n

snapshot:
A Jamieson Brothers Novel

Angie Stanton

rock *and a* hard place

A Jamieson Brothers Novel

HARPER TEEN

An Imprint of HarperCollinsPublishers

HarperTeen is an imprint of HarperCollins Publishers.

Rock and a Hard Place
Copyright © 2013 by Angie Stanton

Library of Congress Cataloging-in-Publication Data
Stanton, Angie.
  Rock and a hard place : A Jamieson brothers novel / by Angie
Stanton. — First edition.
    pages cm
  Summary: Left in small-town Wisconsin with a controlling aunt
after her mother's death, Libby is very unhappy until she meets Peter
and sparks fly, but when she learns that he is a rock star with his own
family problems, her life changes forever.
  ISBN 978-0-06-227254-6 (pbk. bdg.)
  [1. Dating (Social customs)—Fiction. 2. Family problems—Fiction.
3. Singers—Fiction. 4. Rock music—Fiction. 5. Celebrities—Fiction.
6. Aunts—Fiction. 7. Wisconsin—Fiction.] I. Title.
PZ7.S793247Roc 2013   2013010977
[Fic]—dc23   CIP
                                                                     AC

Typography by Laura DiSiena
13 14 15 16 17   CG/RRDH   10 9 8 7 6 5 4 3 2 1
❖
First Edition

For my brother Pat,
thanks for the memories.
This one's for you!

rock *and a* hard place

1

Libby watched the cars zip by on the highway, longing for her dad's SUV with out-of-state plates to drive up and put her life back together. From her spot under an ancient oak, she spied a red SUV exiting the interstate and turning the opposite direction.

She sighed and tried to refocus on the sketch pad in her lap and the wildflowers she'd stuffed in a soda can. But instead, she traced the scars on her palm with the tip of her drawing pencil. If only she could wash the marks away along with the memories of that tragic day. She wiped her palm against her jeans, but only the pencil marks disappeared.

She focused on her drawing and rubbed the side of her pencil on the page, shading a leaf. A rumble caught her attention, and she glanced up; a large, gleaming bus turned off the exit and onto the county road toward her.

The shiny silver-and-black exterior and darkened windows of the vehicle made it look like some sort of VIP ride or maybe a tour bus.

The bus approached the nature preserve and turned in. In all the months she'd come to Parfrey's Glen, cars rarely pulled in, and she liked it that way. She thought of Parfrey's Glen as her own secret place where she could get lost in her thoughts.

The rumble grew louder as the enormous bus turned and pulled to a stop in the gravel parking lot on the far side of the clearing. She waited for the door to open and reveal the famous person within. Maybe it would be some country singer. Her mom loved country music and had always dreamt of going to a big concert. But it never happened.

A moment later the door opened, and Libby's hopes were dashed. Her quiet nature preserve had been invaded. By teenage boys.

A trio of noisy guys poured out. The first leapt from the top step and landed several feet out on the dirt, followed closely by another. The last twirled a Frisbee on his finger as he descended.

She watched them undetected from her spot under the tree, an eavesdropper on this group of loud, young strangers.

The Frisbee sailed through the warm September air as one of the guys raced to catch it. A man and woman exited the bus, their arms loaded with picnic supplies. The woman walked to a sunny spot of grass, set down her load, and spread out a couple of colorful blankets.

They were just a family; okay, a rich family. But no one famous.

Libby enjoyed a perfect view of the group. Their interaction and happy banter reminded her of her own family and made her heartsick.

Her drawing forgotten, she soaked in their every move.

One of the boys turned around, providing her with a clean line of view. He tilted his head to the side and pushed away a lock of sun-kissed hair. A tiny thrill flipped in her stomach. He held an iPod and mini speakers, and loud music filled the air.

"Peter, turn it down," the man hollered as he set up lawn chairs.

"Dad, come on, you never let me play it loud." Peter grinned. He adjusted the volume and set the speakers down.

"Real funny. Now get out of here before I put you to work."

Peter darted through the long grass toward the other two boys, his movements swift and athletic. Libby's eyes trailed his every move.

"Garrett, over here," he yelled.

The Frisbee flew smoothly through the air. Peter leapt high and caught it. "Oh yeah, baby," he bragged, dancing as if it were a touchdown.

He flung it back, his body grace in motion, this time to the boy first out of the bus. This one appeared younger. His hair was a mop of loose dark curls and he wore a constant grin. They continued to torpedo the disk at one another and trash talk in the hot sun of early fall. Occasionally, Peter would do some crazy move to the music playing in the background. Libby stifled a giggle.

Peter suddenly glanced her way.

Uh-oh.

"Heads up," the grinning boy yelled as the Frisbee sped toward the unsuspecting Peter.

Peter ducked as it whistled by and landed not far from Libby. He looked straight at her. Every emotion she wore felt exposed. He jogged over and grabbed the Frisbee from the grass, and he whipped the disc back. He turned around and grinned as he sauntered to where she sat against the giant oak. He plopped down in the unmowed grass, his chest rising heavily.

"Hey." He looked at her with curiosity. "Whatcha doing?"

Libby's mouth went dry as this great-looking guy stretched out before her. Apparently, he expected her to respond. Her tongue felt numb.

A year ago, she would have been comfortable with him. Now, that confidence was a distant memory. These days, guys—anyone really—rarely talked to her anymore. Libby was an outsider to the kids in Rockville, which was fine with her. She had been left in this crummy town and preferred to be alone. It was easier. She'd grown comfortable with solitude, except for now. She prayed for her former confidence to come back.

Libby held the sketch pad as a shield. "Uh, drawing," she uttered.

"Oh." He lay in the grass propped up on a muscular arm. He watched her with casual interest, as his breath came back. He was clearly nothing like the guys at Rockville High School.

"Are you drawing those?" He pointed at the wildflowers sticking haphazardly out of a diet soda can.

"Yeah," she answered softly. "It's really dumb, though," she added, trying to sound normal and not like the insecure girl she'd become. She pulled back and forth at the pendant around her neck.

"Why's it dumb?" His deep blue eyes gazed at her.

She shrugged. "It just is. It doesn't mean anything—it's just something to do." She pressed the pencil hard against the pad and broke the lead.

"Can I see it?" Peter reached for the pad.

Libby's face heated. "I don't know. It's really nothing to look at." She pulled the bound papers close; her fist gripped the pencil tight.

When she didn't offer him the drawing, he moved next to her. He leaned close and took the pad, and his fingers brushed against hers. He sat so near, their legs bumped.

She wanted to reach out and touch him. His blond hair was still streaked by summer sun and hung past his eyebrows and over his eyes. He smelled good. Like shampoo and dryer sheets.

He studied the drawing, then wrinkled his brow as if it wasn't what he expected. He pushed the hair out of his eyes and looked sideways at her. She noticed a touch of razor stubble on his jaw.

"It's not of me," he said, looking embarrassed.

"Why would it be?"

"Well, you've been sitting here watching us, so I figured you must be drawing one of us, too." He handed back the drawing, a bit sheepish.

"Wow. Kind of full of yourself, aren't you?" she teased, feeling brave for a moment. "Sorry to disappoint, but it's just a bunch of wildflowers."

Libby couldn't get over this guy sitting so close. He moved right into her space as if it was no big deal, but it was. She struggled to sit still and not stare at him as her pulse raced.

He studied her, then shook his head.

"Well, it's not very good," he declared, but the corner of his mouth turned up as he fought back a grin. His eyes sparkled.

"Now you're just being mean," she teased again, surprising herself.

She scooted a few inches away to recover from the

awkwardness of being so close. Plus, this way she could sit and look straight at him. He had great eyes.

"Sorry, that's the best I could come up with. You're right. I was mean," he said. "Not a good start here. Let's begin again." He laughed, then leaned forward and held out his hand.

"Hi, I'm Peter."

She looked from his outstretched hand to his friendly face. Happiness wrapped around her like a warm blanket. She couldn't remember the last time she'd had so much fun, and this guy, Peter, with his careless good looks and confident attitude, made her stomach flip.

"Hi, Peter. I'm Libby."

They shook hands and smiled. His hand felt warm and strong.

"So, Libby, do you come here often?"

She rolled her eyes at the lame question. "Yeah, pretty often. Mostly on the weekends." Every chance she got was more like it. Anything to get away from the confines of the house.

"So you must live around here." He looked around for nearby homes.

Libby didn't want him to notice the run-down farmhouse in the distance, so she just nodded. She didn't associate herself with the house, its owner, or even the town.

"What's with the über bus? You on vacation?" She twisted her pendant on its thin leather cord.

"Not really. We live in it when we're on tour." He raised an eyebrow, aware of her not-so-smooth change of topic.

"What do you mean 'tour'? Like a vacation tour of the country?"

He laughed. "No, actually, we're on tour promoting our album, *Triple Threat*," he said with pride in his voice.

"Your family is in a band?"

"It's not my whole family, just my two brothers and me."

His demeanor changed, but she couldn't put her finger on why. She looked across the way to his brothers and furrowed her brow. "You are not. You're making it up." She could tell he was trying to impress her.

"No, really, we've had the band for over two years now."

"Sure you have." She eyed him, not believing a word. They were too young. They must all still be in high school. Plus, they looked nothing like members of a band. She didn't know exactly what guys in a band would look like, but certainly not like these guys.

"I'm telling the truth." He sat back and laughed again.

"So where do you play?" She pierced him with a stare. She'd catch him in his own lie. "You look too young for the bar scene. Do you play weddings?"

A coy expression covered Peter's face. "Uh, no, nothing like that. It's more public places."

"Like parks or fairs?" That she might believe.

"Yeah, something like that."

"Okay, if you say so." She shrugged. "Then you get to

drive around and see lots of different places? I'd do that in an instant, if I could." Anything to escape life here.

"The sights are great, but it can get claustrophobic with five people crammed in one giant tin can for days at a time. You'd hate it."

"Maybe, but I'd be willing to make the sacrifice to get outta here." A tightness in her chest occurred whenever she thought of her trapped existence.

"What's wrong with here?" He twirled a long blade of grass between his fingers.

Where to begin? Nothing about this place fit. It was all wrong. She didn't belong here and never would. But she wasn't about to explain her screwed-up life to Peter. "Just . . . everything."

"Okay, that tells me a lot." He smiled, gazing straight into her eyes. Her stomach turned upside down. "You want to elaborate?"

"No." She swallowed and looked away. "So what's the name of your band?"

"You like to change the subject." He grinned.

She noticed how his eyes sparkled each time he smiled. "So?"

"Jamieson. Our band is called Jamieson." He watched her closely, then asked, "Ever heard of us?"

"Should I have? It doesn't sound familiar."

"Really?" He wore a look of disbelief. "You've never heard of us?"

"No, do you play around here? We have a park pavilion that has groups sometimes. Is that why you stopped in Rockville?"

"No, we haven't played around here." The corner of his mouth turned up. "Don't you listen to the radio or watch TV?"

She sighed. She didn't want him to think she was an idiot. "Of course. Mostly country music, though. I don't recall ever hearing of a band called Jamieson."

"We're not country. Not even close." He shook his head. "And TV?" he asked.

Libby shook her head no. "I don't watch TV too often. Let's just say I get really good grades. And I love nature. That's why I come here so often. What's your reason for stopping?" She could tell that now he was the one having trouble believing her story.

"Whenever we drive through Wisconsin, we stop here because my mom likes how private it is. You know how moms are. Anytime she can find a spot that's surrounded by nature and not all highway, she puts it on the schedule."

Libby glossed over the mom comment. She didn't want to think of her mom. She missed her so much, her heart hurt. "You've been here before?"

"Quite a few times, actually."

Of the dozens of times she'd come to Parfrey's, she'd never seen them. How odd that today they would meet.

This news warmed her insides. She wondered how many times in this last lonely year they'd just missed each other coming and going.

"Hey, Petey, who's your girlfriend?" one of Peter's brothers yelled as he moved toward them with a cocky walk and hooded eyes. He appeared older, a little shorter than Peter, and not nearly as good-looking. He stared at her.

"That's Garrett," he said under his breath. "Ignore him. He can be a jerk."

"Lover boy, Mom said it's time to eat."

Libby pulled her knees in and hugged them. She couldn't see any resemblance between Garrett and Peter.

"I'm coming." Peter got to his feet and turned toward Libby. "I've gotta go, but maybe I'll see you later."

She smiled and nodded. She'd love to see him, more than he'd ever know.

Libby checked her watch. "Oh my God, I didn't realize how late it's getting. I've gotta go, too." If she didn't leave right now, she'd get the third degree. She flipped the sketch pad closed and gathered her belongings.

"Here." Peter extended a hand to her, his face kind and close.

"Thanks." She grasped his strong hand and stood up, relishing the touch of his skin.

"It was fun talking to you. I wish I'd bumped into you sooner," he said.

Was he actually disappointed to see her go?

"Who knows? Maybe I'll see you again someday." He smiled.

"Maybe." She couldn't imagine it happening, but for the first time in months she felt hopeful—happy, even.

"Have fun on your tour." She dumped the weeds and wildflowers onto the ground. "I've gotta go."

She hesitated for a moment, not wanting this to end. It had been a very long time since she'd relaxed and hung out with anyone, let alone a nice guy.

"Well, bye." She ran down the trail into the woods. Once in the thick of the trees, she turned back. Peter stood in the same spot, holding one of the wildflowers she'd left behind. He waved. She waved back, then disappeared into the woods.

Libby took the long way, so Peter wouldn't see where she lived.

• • •

Libby braced herself as she approached the beat-up old farm-house. It loomed forgotten on acres of rich farmland and wooded areas. Most of the land was leased to a farmer, who benefited from the fertile soil. From what she could tell, this was her aunt's sole method of income. The rest of the property, barn, and outbuildings sat abandoned with a collection of broken-down cars littering the yard. The odor of leaking oil and rusted metal clung to the air. A vegetable garden had once flourished, but that must have been years ago.

She didn't know why her aunt had let it all fall apart, but her parents always said Aunt Marge struggled with demons early in life and never recovered from the fight. Libby heaved a sigh and inserted her key into the lock on the paint-chipped door.

Upon entering, the familiar smell of stale smoke and reeking trash filled the air. The television blared in the next room, confirming her aunt's presence. Libby hoped to sneak upstairs unnoticed.

"Don't forget to lock the door behind you. We can't be taking any chances," the gritty voice of her aunt hollered from the sickeningly sweet smoke-filled living room. "People are getting murdered in their beds every day."

"It's locked," Libby said, resigned. The house was dark, as always. Aunt Marge kept the curtains closed, as if anyone would want to watch a middle-aged woman drink and watch television all day.

"Come in here."

Libby dropped her backpack at the foot of the steps and dragged her feet as she entered the living room. Aunt Marge reclined in an upholstered chair, her feet on a mismatched ottoman. A dented TV tray served as her coffee table, cluttered with a lighter, a pack of cigarettes, a bottle of whiskey, and a dirty glass.

"What's wrong?" her aunt demanded while clenching a cigarette between her thin, stained lips.

"Nothing," she mumbled, pushing her long hair behind an ear as she tolerated the inspection.

"You're not lying to me, are you?" Aunt Marge's eyes narrowed. "I hate liars."

"No, I would never lie to you. I just have a lot of home-work."

She grunted in reply. "There's groceries on the counter if you're hungry. Now get upstairs and finish your work. You know I won't tolerate laziness. You prove to those school people you're doing just fine. I don't need them snooping around here again." She picked up the television remote and started snapping it at the television, effectively dismissing her.

Libby made her way through the cluttered house into the kitchen. On the edge of the counter, next to piles of dirty dishes and old junk mail, sat a torn grocery bag. She began pulling things out. A bag of cheese popcorn, a box of granola bars, a bag of red licorice, and a warm package of sandwich meat. At the bottom she found a six-pack of soda and three candy bars.

She placed the soda and unappetizing sandwich meat on a crusty metal shelf in the refrigerator, grabbed the pop-corn and a candy bar, and went upstairs with her backpack. It was always a relief to leave Aunt Marge behind. With any luck, she wouldn't hear from her again today. Hopefully, she'd drink herself into a stupor and fall asleep in her sunken chair.

Once inside her room, Libby pushed the door shut, closing out the ugliness below. She set her things on the neatly made bed. The worn bedspread featured snags and small tears, but she kept it and everything in the room as clean as possible. She'd given up on keeping the downstairs clean months ago, but here she could keep things the way she liked.

She picked up the small, framed picture of her family. Her mom, dad, and little sister, Sarah, along with a former version of herself, smiled brightly. The photo was taken while on a rafting trip out west two years earlier. Their arms hung comfortably on one another's shoulders, reminding her of the love they'd shared. Libby traced their faces with her finger and wondered when her dad would come back for her.

She returned the photo to its place on her dresser and moved to the two large windows, raising them a few inches. Cool air blew in, making her room feel better. Outside, across the fields, the rear entrance to the preserve was in perfect view. The spot she'd met Peter. She pulled a chair near the window and propped her book on her lap as she began doing homework, checking too often for Peter and the silver tour bus.

2

The next day, Libby walked solo through the crowded halls of Rockville High School.

"Libby, could you come in here for a minute?" Miss Orman called out in a friendly voice. When Libby started at Rockville, Miss Orman immediately made it her mission to help her. Sometimes it was a little overwhelming, but Libby didn't mind; she liked the woman, and she always meant well.

"Yeah, sure." Libby hiked her backpack higher on her shoulder and entered the tiny office. It was always nice to hang with Miss Orman. Posters of positive thinking with adorable kittens lined the wall; a bulletin board overflowed with official letters about DARE and the school dress code as well as a couple of long strips of student photos.

She dropped her pack on the floor and sank into an

orange metal chair squeezed in next to an overflowing bookcase.

Miss Orman settled behind her desk in her tan dress pants and stylish heels. She leaned toward Libby with sincere eyes. "So how are things?"

"Fine." Libby offered her standard answer.

"Tell me, how are your classes going? You're carrying a heavy course load."

"Calculus is tough, but I'm doing okay."

"That's good, and how about at home? Anything you want to share with me about your aunt?" Her face showed compassion.

Miss Orman was the only person who had a clue about her horrible life with Aunt Marge. Libby would never consider that dilapidated old house a home. There was nothing of hers there, other than a few token items. "I get by. I just try to stay out of the way."

Miss Orman forced a smile, but her lips were pressed tight. "Sounds like a good plan, but promise you'll let me know if you have any problems."

Libby nodded.

Miss Orman's phone rang loudly on the desk. She ignored it and then leaned in and asked, "Have you thought any more about college?"

"Yeah, but I'm going to wait for my dad to come back before I pick a school. We're going to check out campuses together." Libby and her dad had been planning to travel east to visit colleges since she had turned fourteen.

"That's wonderful," Miss Orman said, but her smile didn't reach her eyes this time. "Are you making any new friends?" Her voice sounded hopeful.

"I'm fine, really. I prefer to be on my own." It was easier this way. If she made friends, they'd want to hear all the details of her tragic life, and she didn't want to talk about that. Plus, she only planned on staying here until her dad returned.

"I wish you'd open yourself up to the students here. I think you could make some good friends." Miss Orman gave her a pointed look. "You are a gifted young lady with a lot to offer."

Miss Orman's support made Libby feel just a little bit protected, like maybe her mom was still here.

"It's okay. They all think I'm like my aunt, the town crazy woman." Libby couldn't believe how just a couple of events had turned her from the popular girl at her old school into an outsider here.

"I don't want you walking around believing that. You just need to make an effort to get to know them better. What happened to you working at the concession stand during the football game?"

"My aunt said no. She thinks I'll be corrupted by all the kids who drink." Libby rewarded Miss Orman with a half smile.

"Well, we'll come up with something else." Her counselor curled a lock of hair behind her ear.

Libby paused for a moment. If Miss Orman was so concerned, maybe she should mention Peter.

"Actually, I met someone," Libby blurted. Miss Orman looked up, visibly surprised. "At Parfrey's Glen." Her pulse rate jumped just thinking about it.

"Oh? Tell me about it." Miss Orman scooted her chair closer.

"I was just sitting there when this huge bus pulled in. It was this family that travels all around. One of them, this guy"—her face warmed, but she ignored it—"he came over and talked to me for a long time. It was really sweet."

"Well, that's terrific!" Miss Orman leaned back and slapped her hand on the desk. "So who is he?"

"His name is Peter, and he is so nice. He and his brothers are in a band, and they perform all over." She couldn't contain her joy as she recalled their afternoon together.

"What were they doing in Rockville?"

"Just stopping for a break, I guess. When I left, they were having a big picnic. They weren't performing here. I don't know where they were going, but he said they're promoting their new CD."

Miss Orman nodded. "Wow, that's impressive. So, what's the name of their band?"

"He told me the name, but I can't remember." Libby looked toward the ceiling and tried to recall. "Something like Double Danger, I don't know." How could she have forgotten already?

Miss Orman pursed her lips.

"He said they're touring the country," Libby offered, to make up for her lapse in memory. She realized how far-fetched the story sounded.

"Where do they play next?" Miss Orman asked, her tone doubtful.

"Um, well, I'm not sure, actually." She shrugged and chewed at her lip.

Miss Orman smiled, but this time it didn't look genuine. "Well, that's still great. Too bad we don't know who the mystery man is. Maybe you'll see him again?"

"I don't know. I doubt it." Libby tried to predict how she and Peter would ever hook up again. Most likely it would never happen. "Probably not." Her head dropped, and she focused on the floor. Suddenly, all she wanted was to escape this tiny office.

Miss Orman reached out and patted her arm. "I think it's wonderful you met someone, even if you never see him again. Just think what a great memory you have. Heck, maybe he'll make it big someday and you'll recognize him on TV."

Libby smiled wanly, her spirits deflated. It was all basically a dream. A really great dream that no one would ever believe. "Well, I better go." She picked up her backpack and boosted it onto her shoulder.

"Hey, look on the bright side. Maybe you had a brush with a future star."

With a forced smile, Libby left the office.

• • •

Heart-pumping music blared through the New York City photo studio. Giant fans created windblown effects for the action shots.

"Peter, lower your chin. Good!" James, the photographer, yelled over the music. James moved constantly to catch every angle possible. Photo shoots tended to go long, and today was no exception.

The bright lights burned down as flashes popped. Peter always got a kick out of all the primping for the shoots and the goofy way photographers posed them for the perfect look.

"Adam, this way. Hold your concentration! Remember, you are a hard-core rocker."

Adam and Peter broke into laughter. "You can't say stuff like that if you want us to keep a straight face," Adam replied, and pushed his fingers through his mop of curly hair.

The guys walked around the set and laughed to shake off pent-up energy.

"You guys are killing me." The photographer lowered his camera while the hairstylist stepped in to fix Adam's hair.

"Ya know, it's hard to be 'hard-core' anything when

you travel with your mom, and she's always nagging you to brush your teeth and pick up your clothes," Peter added.

James couldn't resist laughing. "Okay, this is the last set. Let's pull it together for a few more minutes. Remember, this is for *Rolling Stone*; it's worth the effort."

Peter couldn't get over the fact that Jamieson would grace the cover of the legendary magazine. Their popularity shot through the roof this past year. They were living the dream.

"Okay, guys, I want you to think 'brooding rocker'— think Kurt Cobain or Jim Morrison." James raised the camera to his eye.

The brothers, always consummate professionals, fell back into place, doing their best to follow direction even though they were slaphappy after three wardrobe and set changes.

"You do realize they both died of drug overdoses," Garrett added.

"Yeah, and you should be very sad about their wasted talent. Now show it to me on your faces," the photographer said with a pointed look.

The threesome switched gears and slid easily into character. Peter thought about his dream to be a career musician, not just part of a boy band with the shelf life of a ripe banana. Jamieson had been fortunate with great reviews and success beyond his dreams, but this was a fickle industry. He wanted to have a lifelong career like the rock greats before him. Their careers had legs, and so would his. Giving a serious expression wasn't so hard after all.

Twenty minutes later, the primping and posing ended and they headed off set.

"Guys, grab some lunch while we go over details for the rest of the day," their middle-aged manager, Wally, instructed.

A few minutes later, with their plates piled high, they, along with their entourage, gathered around a large table in a meeting room at the studio.

"We have another busy day ahead of us," Wally said, scratching his balding head. He opened a binder filled with tour information. "The CD signing begins in one hour. We'll bring you in through the side fire exit."

"That's good," Adam interrupted. "We'll know where to get out when the fire starts. 'Cause we're so hot!"

"You are such an idiot," Peter said.

"Security is already in place," Wally continued, looking at Roger, their personal security manager. "So, hopefully, we won't have any problems like in Miami. Roger has been working with store management. You have two hours to get the crowd through the signing. We can't go long because you have a live interview with WABC-TV at four. Sound check follows that. Oh yeah, tonight we've got a kid from Make-A-Wish who will shadow you until after the concert. Anybody want to take lead on that?"

"Boy or girl?" Garrett asked, wiping mustard off his fingers and onto Adam's sleeve.

"Don't you have respect for anything?" Adam shook his head, dabbed at the smear of mustard with a napkin, and tossed it into Garrett's soda.

"Let's see." Wally ignored them and looked over his notes. "It's a twelve-year-old boy. His name is Jacob."

"Nah, I'll pass, but when you get an eighteen-year-old girl, she's all mine," Garrett said.

"I'll take him." Peter signaled, his mouth stuffed with turkey and cheese. He grabbed his soda, took a long drag, and swallowed. "What's he got?" Seeing kids suffer broke Peter's heart. He remembered his own hospitalization for appendicitis at age fourteen. He'd been terrified. He couldn't imagine how scary it was for kids who were really sick.

"Some kind of cancer. It doesn't look good," answered Wally. "Roger, anything you want to add?"

Roger, their trusty bodyguard, was tall and built like a giant oak. Whenever they were out and about, he became a constant companion. Peter loved having him around. Roger had served in Iraq for a while and didn't want to settle into a regular job when he returned home. Working for Jamieson was anything but regular.

"Yeah, the crowds at the record store are huge, and the entry space is tight. We're gonna have to make a fast in and out. No time for shout-outs or photos." Roger stared at Adam. "And, yes, that means you, Adam."

Adam loved to let the girls fawn over him, and it drove Peter nuts. He held the group up constantly with his friendly banter and willingness to pose for photos with every single fan. Roger constantly had to shoo the girls away. Probably his most difficult job on the tour.

Peter loved the fans for their enthusiasm and support, but that's where it ended. There was a fine line with fans, and he wasn't interested in crossing it. It was impossible to connect with a girl who'd screamed your name moments before and then trembled with nervousness—or worse yet, cried—the whole time she talked to you. Touring wasn't a normal way to make friends. He wanted to meet someone the old-fashioned way, not under the guise of fame.

Peter thought of Libby. Meeting her felt normal. No crowds, no cameras, just two people hanging out. She looked so beautiful and relaxed sitting under a tree with her long, blond hair blowing in the autumn breeze. He loved that she didn't know who Jamieson was. Even if she did, he wasn't sure it would make any difference. He wouldn't mind seeing her again.

Wally interrupted Peter's thoughts. "We've got a busy day, so let's stay on task. That's all I've got." He snapped the binder closed.

• • •

After hours of hand-cramping signatures, a limo whisked the brothers, their publicist, manager, and bodyguard to

Madison Square Garden, where the roadies finished their stage setup. Including lasers and pyrotechnics, it took a crew of over thirty more than twelve hours to create the enormous stage and set.

The interview team from WABC was in place and ready to film. A half hour in hair and makeup and the Jamieson brothers were ready to roll tape.

They sat in matching directors' chairs and faced the interviewer, Andrea Jacobs, an attractive, young redhead who wore masterfully applied thick makeup. She probably looked better without it.

Two cameras were set among the many lights. The news producer stood close by and began the countdown. "Five, four . . ." He signaled the last three counts by pointing his finger on each beat.

"This is Andrea Jacobs, reporting live from Madison Square Garden. Joining me today is the chart-topping teen sensation, Jamieson."

Peter hated it when the press reduced their sound to a teenybopper boy band. The camera panned across each of the brothers and then back to include all three as a group.

"In a few short hours, this arena will overflow with thousands of teenagers and adults, too! What is your secret to attracting such a diverse crowd?"

Peter lifted his microphone. "It's really the music. Our sound appeals to a wide audience."

"No argument there," Andrea responded. "Your latest single is climbing the charts at record speed. Is it true you write your own music?"

"Actually, Peter is the genius behind our music. Adam and I contribute, but Peter's instincts are on the pulse of what's great," Garrett answered.

Despite Garrett's many flaws, he always gave Peter credit for their songwriting success. Peter appreciated it.

"That's incredible for someone your age. You've written some amazing hits. How about Adam and Garrett? Do you have a specialty?"

"Adam is master on the guitar," Peter offered. "Without him, we would be a mediocre bar band."

"And Garrett?" Andrea asked. She licked her puffed-up, gloss-covered lips as she eyed Garrett in a way that made Peter uncomfortable.

"I play bass guitar. I also work on the business side of things. I make sure we stay on top of the trends and work to come up with ways to remain successful."

Peter nodded in agreement. Garrett was annoying, yet effective.

"You are a group of talented young men, mature beyond your age." She directed her comments straight to Garrett. He gave her a sly smile.

It was impossible not to mature quickly when you carried a multimillion-dollar business on your back. The livelihood of dozens of people relied on their success.

"We opened our email up to Jamieson fans to ask some questions. Here's what some of your fans want to know," Andrea said. "Who is bossiest?"

"Garrett!" Adam and Peter said at the same time. The guy was a total control freak.

"Hey, someone's gotta tell you what to do," Garrett said.

"Who has the most girlfriends?" she asked with interest.

"Garrett!" they answered again. Garrett shrugged. He enjoyed the perks of playing in a band.

"Who is the leader of the group?"

"Peter," the other two said in unison.

Peter wasn't sure why that was. Taking the lead onstage seemed as natural as breathing. He felt connected to the crowd.

"Who is the goof-off?"

"Are you kidding? It's all Adam," Peter answered.

Adam shrugged, never a care in the world. He was always seen with either a camera or a guitar in his hands.

"Okay, who is the shyest?"

Garrett and Adam looked straight at Peter. No words necessary.

"Really, now that surprises me," Andrea said. "You write the music and lead the band, yet you're the shy one?"

Peter tried not to squirm. "I don't know that I'm shy, but I keep to myself more than Garrett and Adam. They're more outgoing. I like to spend time alone."

"Aw, the brooding artist. No wonder your music is so

successful," she responded. "This last one is for each of you. What is your idea of the perfect girl?"

"I'd say it's a girl who makes me laugh," Adam said with a smile.

The camera moved to Peter.

"I'd like someone who is interested in me and not all the other crazy parts that come with success," Peter said.

"I'm looking for a beautiful girl who loves to party." Garrett looked at her pointedly.

The camera refocused on Andrea. "There you have it, girls. Now you know what it takes to attract one of these charming young men. Thank you for your time, guys, and have a great concert tonight. It's sold out, but I'm one of the lucky ones who hold a backstage pass." She looked at Garrett with silent meaning.

Peter was happy to see the interview end before Garrett embarrassed them all. As he followed his brothers offstage, he thought of Libby. He bet she would never act like the reporter. Libby seemed interested in him and not everything else that came with being in a band. He wouldn't mind running into her again and finding out for sure.

3

$\mathcal{A}$ few days later, Libby sat on a giant outcropping of rock at Parfrey's Glen that reached out over the rushing creek. The warm September breeze blew gently through the trees and swept a leaf into the water below. Her eyes followed it, and as it floated along, she pondered the events of the past week. Miss Orman had tried to cheer her up after Libby couldn't support her story about Peter. It all seemed unreal. If she hadn't experienced it herself, she wouldn't believe it, either. Famous people didn't just appear out of nowhere, especially not in Rockville.

But Peter had appeared. And she had spent time with him. He was beautiful and perfect, and she couldn't remember the last time she'd felt so happy. The best part was that he didn't know about her life or that she lived with her crazy aunt Marge. Peter didn't know that her dad's grief was so strong, he'd brought Libby to Wisconsin and left her at his sister-in-law's house before driving off into the depths of depression.

The noise of wind rushing through the trees increased. It sounded like the roar of the nearby highway. Libby lay on the large stone slab, her back warmed by the sun-heated rock. She gazed at the movement of the tree branches overhead as they bent and swayed in the wind. The leaves were a patchwork of green, yellow, and orange. Fall had created a beautiful scene. Her thoughts returned to Peter and how wonderful her life would be if he were in it.

A shadow moved over her and blocked the sun. She jerked onto her elbows to discover the intrusion. People rarely came to this part of the preserve.

"Are you cutting class?" Peter stood before her, a broad smile on his face and the familiar hair falling in his eyes.

"Oh my God." Libby popped up from her spot. "What are you doing here?"

She never thought she'd see him again. Hoped, yes, but not in her wildest dreams did she believe it could happen. She stared, her mouth agape.

His T-shirt hugged him snug across the chest and shoulders, revealing strong arms. His jeans hung low, his thumbs looped in the top of his pockets. She looked at his handsome face. His eyes sparkled with mischief as the breeze tossed his hair.

"Mom really likes this spot, and now so do I." He grinned and a gorgeous dimple appeared. "We're heading up to Minneapolis for some taping."

"Guess it's my lucky day," she bubbled.

"Guess so." With a devilish grin, he raised an eyebrow.

Her stomach did a flip. "How much time do you have?" She got up and wiped her dusty hands on her jeans, then slid them into her back pockets. She stood a few feet away, not sure what to do.

"As long as we want," Peter answered.

She beamed.

"Well, an hour, at the most," he corrected, another cute smirk in the corner of his mouth.

"We better not waste time then." They faced each other, a momentary pause and an instant of awkwardness. Libby refused to let this opportunity pass. She broke the silence. "Have you seen the rock formations at the back of the glen?"

"No, but I'd love to."

"It's this way." She tilted her head toward the trail and fought the urge to squeal with joy.

They followed the path through the rocky ravine, the walls progressively greener with rich moss. Every so often, water trickled down the sides, flowing into the stream they walked along. Peter moved next to her, and she tried not to look at him too often.

"You never answered my question," Peter said, stepping over a sharp rock.

"What was that?" Libby glanced up.

"Are you cutting school? It's a Wednesday afternoon,

and where I come from we go to school on Wednesdays."

"No, it's teacher in-service. We get a Wednesday afternoon off once a month so the teachers can meet and talk about how horrible today's youth are."

"You must be at the top of their list." He grinned and held his hand out to help her over the large rocks.

"You have no idea." She placed her hand in his, reveling at his warmth in the cool ravine.

Gravel crunched beneath their feet as they made their way along the crooked path. Occasionally, he bumped her shoulder playfully, as if he wanted to make sure she was still there. Something about him fit. He didn't ask too many questions or judge the things she told him. It had been a long time since someone had accepted her.

"Tell me again why your family comes here?" She wanted him to say it was so he could see her and then promise they would be here every day.

"They like this spot," Peter said, jumping easily from one boulder to another. "It's close to the interstate, and we pass this way a lot when we're traveling between Chicago and Minneapolis. Mom is always trying to make us feel normal and keep us grounded."

"But you are normal."

"Are you kidding?" He gave her a look of disbelief. "We're far from it."

"But you have a mom and dad and a big family that spends lots of time together." To her, they seemed like the most magical, perfect family, almost as good as hers had once been.

"We spend too much time together." He ran his fingers through his long bangs, pushing them out of the way. "I can't tell you how often I wish I could ditch my family. I never get any privacy."

"That is one thing I have a ton of." She looked out at the creek as it rushed over age-old rocks. Her days were filled with solitude. But sometimes she wished someone special cared about her. It might be nice to have a friend to keep her from spending too much time alone, or to drag her into a game of Frisbee, or to talk to about nothing at all.

Peter's voice brought her out of her silent lament.

"I'd trade my little brother, Adam, for more privacy any day."

Their eyes connected, giving her another jolt. She thought of her younger sister, Sarah. Libby would trade anything for one more day with her. She swallowed down the hurt she felt whenever she thought of her.

"I shouldn't complain," he continued. "But once in a while, it'd be nice not to have every minute of my life planned."

"What do you mean?" She hopped from one large rock to the next, putting those thoughts behind her.

He considered her carefully. "You really don't get it, do you?"

Her backbone stiffened. "Of course I do." She hated being talked down to. She left his side and moved ahead, jumping from rock to rock as she crossed the stream.

"Don't get all stuck-up on me, but do you really understand what I do?"

"Yeah, you sing with your brothers. You travel around in your bus and perform. I'm not a total moron." Why did he have to show his jerk side? Everything had been perfect.

"I didn't say you were a moron, but there's a lot more to it than that." Peter easily leapt over the rocks to reach her. He held her arm to slow her down. The stream rushed by noisily; the earthy smells of moss and ferns surrounded them.

"Okay, for example, we just came from New York, where we were on *Rock Hits Live*."

She stared blankly, arms crossed, refusing to admit her ignorance.

"You don't know what that is?" He shook his head in disbelief. "It's a live music interview show. Do you ever watch TV?" he asked.

Libby huffed a sigh of irritation. "No. I haven't watched TV for over a year. Okay?" Which was true, Aunt Marge's ancient set was always turned to one home shopping network or another.

"Really?" he responded.

She could see the unasked question behind his eyes.

"Okay, listen," he said, determined to help her understand. "We just came out with our third CD."

"Yeah, well, anyone can make a CD. We have a media class where kids create them for extra credit." Ahead, an enormous boulder dominated the end of the trail; the creek poured out on each side. Libby climbed over the surrounding rocks, reached the top, and sat. Peter followed.

"You're right, it's not that hard to put together a CD. But we've got a major recording contract. We spent a month in the studio recording our latest music. We're doing massive publicity for our new CD."

The more he spoke, the more she noticed a serious side to him. This was his life and clearly his passion. Libby's pulse quickened as she listened. It seemed even more impossible he'd be here talking to her.

"Every day is filled with rehearsals, interviews, and appearances. So between all that work and travel, it doesn't leave much time to think, let alone relax."

Peter's concentration moved from Libby for a moment as he noticed their surroundings. They perched on top of a huge boulder in the heart of the glen. Every inch of the steep, rocky sides dripped with silky moss, and ferns poked out their feathery fronds. The moist scent of the glen's lush vegetation filled the air. A cool mist floated around them. This was Libby's magic place.

"This is amazing." Awe colored his voice.

"Yeah, it is. I'm glad you like it." She leaned back on her

hands and inhaled a deep breath of nature's gift. "So, when are you done? When do you go home?" She ran her hand over the cool, gritty rock, afraid to hear the truth.

He flipped his mop of hair out of his face. "We get a couple days to go home to San Antonio here and there, but we're booked solid for the next ten weeks. Then, if everything falls into place, we might be going to Europe for a couple months."

This amazing guy lived his life bigger than her wildest dreams. Maybe she could have thought about travel and making huge plans, but life had delivered a left hook and knocked her off her feet. She wrapped her arms around her knees and held tight.

"Now what's that look for?" he asked, confused.

"Nothing. I just didn't know you were such a big deal." Her lips tightened into a thin line. "I must look really boring to you." She wouldn't meet his eyes. Why was he wasting his time with her?

"I didn't tell you all that to brag, but I figure you should know we're not just another folk group singing on Sundays. Not that there's anything wrong with that. It's just not who we are."

He leaned forward, caught her eye, and refused to look away. "And you're not boring—totally the opposite. It's just that we're always on the go, one rehearsal, taping, or interview after another. All day, every day. We never stop. My dad and Garrett are always plotting and planning the next step of our career." Peter mindlessly rolled a small pebble between his thumb and forefinger.

"Don't you like it?" She searched his eyes.

"Yes, I love it! Are you kidding?" He tossed the pebble to the water below. "I'm living my greatest fantasy. Every day I wake up amazed all this is happening. But it gets exhausting, and sometimes I just want privacy, time to be alone."

He gazed into her eyes. "But times like this, where I'm doing what I want, like sitting with you . . ." He bumped shoulders with her again. "They're the best."

Libby nudged him back. "See, not every minute of your day is planned."

He took her hand and gave it a warm squeeze. She rewarded him with a shy smile. "So what's your favorite part of the band?"

"The best part is performing. I could sing onstage all night. There's such a connection to the music and the audience. It's total euphoria."

They sat atop the giant rock engulfed in the misty, cool beauty of the glen. They relaxed, content in each other's company. Peter ran his thumb over her fingers. Suddenly, he paused and turned her hand over.

"What's this?" he asked innocently.

"Nothing." She snatched her hand away, embarrassed.

"No, give it back." He reached out and pulled her hand

back into his two and examined the violent bumps. "What are all these marks?"

Her face heated at his question. "It's nothing." She tried to brush it off, but dread crept in.

"It's not nothing. It looks like cuts." He held tight to her hand as he examined it. "You're not a cutter, are you?" He looked her straight in the eye.

"No! Now let go." She tried to pull her hand away, but he wouldn't release her. Libby's happiness spiraled down, the joy of the day gone.

"Well, what happened?"

She understood why he asked. She might ask the same thing. Peter's expression was honest concern, nothing more.

"They're scars. From a car accident." She bit her lip, not wanting to reveal any more.

"Oh God, that's terrible." He continued to study her permanently marred fingers and palm. "It must have been a really bad accident."

"Yeah, it was," she whispered as the image of the crumpled car and glow of ambulance lights flashed in her mind.

He peeked up at her, past the heavy chunk of hair that covered his eyes. "You know, they look like little starbursts."

"Whatever you say," she replied, not seeing it.

"Give me the other one," he commanded. For some reason, she obeyed and extended her other hand. He examined both palms, lightly trailing his thumb and fingers over the surface of her skin. Shivers ran up her arms.

"No, they're not starbursts." He continued to touch each mark. "They're angel kisses. It's like angels kissed your hands all over." His eyes rose to meet hers. They were filled with kindness and compassion. Something she had felt little of the past year.

Only Peter could turn the violent scars from a devastating accident into something beautiful. He was the sweetest person she'd ever met. Without another word, he lifted first one hand and then the other and softly kissed each little mark on her tender, scarred hands.

Libby's mouth opened in wonder. His warm breath tickled her skin as his lips gently moved. Goose bumps danced up her arms. Never in her life had she felt this way, and she never wanted this moment to end.

Peter looked up, her hands cradled in his, as if it were a perfectly normal thing to do. His eyes, a deep pool of blue, melted into hers. Libby's breath slowed. Today her world was perfect. This beautiful boy held her captive. His expression confirmed he felt the same. They leaned their heads closer, just inches apart.

Libby saw something move out of the corner of her eye. "Ouch! Crap."

They looked up just in time to see Peter's brother, Adam, slip down the side of the boulder, dropping his expensive-looking camera in the process.

"What the . . . ?" Peter exclaimed. They jumped away from each other as if guilty. Adam crouched at the bottom of the large boulder, checking his camera for damage.

"Adam, what the hell are you doing?" Peter yelled, their moment shattered.

"Looking for you, nimrod. Dad's really pissed. You were supposed to be back an hour ago."

"Damn," Peter said under his breath.

Adam resumed his picture-taking, focusing on Libby and Peter.

"Stop it." Peter reached for the camera. "Don't make me break that thing."

"Hey, I've got some great stuff here. This new lens is amazing. I've heard the paparazzi use this type, too. I got it all, Peter, including your nose hairs. You should really trim them." Adam ducked out of Peter's reach before he could get smacked.

"Libby, please excuse my 'little' brother. As you can see, he is an idiot."

"Hi," Libby said, mortified.

Adam flashed her a huge grin.

"Adam here is going to hightail it back to the bus and tell them I'm on my way. That way, I won't have to break his fingers. Right?" Peter stood and glared at his brother.

"Dad would be pretty ticked if you did that. Plus, who'd play lead for you, so you don't go off-key all the time?"

"Libby, can you find me a rock? I need to throw it at Adam."

"Jeez, you really know how to spoil a party," Adam complained.

Peter faked a throw.

"I'm going, I'm going." Adam turned and hurried down the trail, jumping from one large rock to another, occasionally looking back toward them and snapping another picture.

Peter turned to her.

"I'm so sorry. My family is the worst. They drive me nuts."

"It's okay. I don't mind." Libby smiled. She would give anything to have a family again. Especially one like his.

"We better get going. My dad hates to be kept waiting."

They rushed back, covering the ground in a fraction of the time it took to get there. Peter took her hand often to help her over large boulders that blocked the path.

When they arrived at the break in the woods, the engine of the grand tour bus rumbled impatiently.

"This was great," Libby said to Peter. She hated to see it end.

"Hey, we head back down to Chicago on Saturday. I can't promise anything, but I bet I can talk my mom into a stop here. Any chance you could meet me? Can I call you?"

First excitement, then panic hit. Visions of Aunt Marge answering the phone filled her mind. "No, you can't call. I'm sorry." She softened. "But I can be here. I'll wait for you."

"No phone, either, huh?" He winked. "It'll probably be around lunchtime. I'm sorry I can't give you an exact time." He spoke fast, looking to the bus every few seconds. "I'll meet you at that flat rock outcropping where I found you today."

"I'll be there." She would wait all day if need be. Anything for another chance to see Peter.

"I've gotta run. Bye."

"Bye." She watched as Peter jogged easily across the field toward the bus, a smile permanently etched on her face.

4

At school the next day, Mr. Hursley, the computer teacher, gave final instructions to the class.

"Be sure to save your work often. The network has been acting up again, and it would be a shame to have the best homecoming flyer ever designed for Rockville High fall victim to a cyber-death."

He took a cursory lap around the room to make sure everyone was on task. The tap of keyboards in action filled the room. Satisfied, Mr. Hursley eased into his desk chair, adjusted his outdated bifocals, and settled into the sports section.

Libby eyed the people around her. To her right sat Courtney Golding and Allison Smith, two popular girls who believed the world revolved around them. They scooted their chairs close together and whispered under the hum of two dozen computers. Libby heard them discussing their homecoming dresses and what trendy restaurant their dates would take them to. Homecoming was so far off Libby's radar.

On her left slouched basketball star Tom West, his incredibly long legs stretched far beneath the table. He peered toward the teacher's desk, where Mr. Hursley buried himself behind the newspaper. Tom slid in tiny earbuds and began nodding to the beat of unheard music. How Tom manipulated the tiny iPod with his giant hands, Libby couldn't fathom.

With everyone's attention elsewhere, she hunched closer to the keyboard, clicked on the internet icon, and typed in "Google." Instantly, the screen popped up. Most kids spent hours surfing the web. The only time Libby touched a computer was to work on school assignments during class. Aunt Marge would never own something as expensive as a computer; she lived in the Dark Ages. For the first time in many months, Libby was motivated to break the rules a little and play on the web.

Her nerves betrayed her as her hands began to shake. She pulled away from the keyboard as if burned. This was silly. She never broke the rules, and this was so simple. She just wanted to know more about Peter, and the information was just a few keystrokes away.

She took a deep breath and rested her arms on the desk.

Last night lying in bed, she'd remembered his last name. With nervous concentration, she clicked on the SEARCH box and typed PETER JAMIESON.

Seeing his name on screen brought him to life as if he sat right before her. Her hand hovered over the ENTER key. Why was she nervous? She'd worked hard not to care about anything anymore, but now she wanted this so badly, her stomach hurt.

She bit her lower lip, reached out with her right index finger, and pressed ENTER.

4,710,084 items in 0.23 seconds.

Libby's jaw dropped. A list displayed item after item.

She leaned back in the chair, her hand covering her mouth. Over four million hits! This couldn't possibly be right. She clicked on IMAGES, and there it was, his familiar smile over and over.

It made no sense. Why would the boy on the screen want to be her friend? What would a guy like Peter see in her? Was she going nuts? No, she still remembered the touch of his lips on her hands. It was insane!

She leaned forward, oblivious to the world around her, and began to read the headings.

PETER JAMIESON, SONGWRITING GENIUS, STRIKES GOLD WITH NEW ALBUM.

PETER JAMIESON VISITS KIDS AT TULSA CHILDREN'S HOSPITAL.

PETER JAMIESON, LEAD SINGER OF THE BAND JAMIESON,
ROCKS MADISON SQUARE GARDEN.

"Miss Sawyer, that doesn't look anything like a home-coming flyer."

She jumped in her seat, knocking her knee against the table leg, then whipped around. Mr. Hursley stood planted behind her, arms crossed. Libby swallowed.

"Are you finished with your work already, or do you need detention to help get you back on track?" Mr. Hursley didn't mess around.

"No," she responded, her eyes like a deer's in the headlights. The heat in her body rose up her neck to her face, turning it a hot pink. Don't cry.

Basketball boy and the gossip girls watched, entertained to witness her embarrassment, and probably relieved she'd gotten caught messing around instead of them.

Mr. Hursley leaned forward, took the mouse, and closed the web page. Peter vanished from sight. The void on the screen hit like a punch to her gut.

"Let's get back on task, shall we?" He arched an eyebrow.

"Yes, sir," she mumbled, wondering how she could go on with anything now that she knew where to find Peter. Everything about him was so near, only a few keystrokes away.

"I don't want to contact your parents." He paused and

corrected himself. "I'm sorry, I mean your aunt."

Courtney and Allison stared at her, smirking.

Libby couldn't risk Aunt Marge getting a call. The last thing she wanted was to deal with Aunt Marge's hysterics. Libby needed a plan. She had to find a way to spend time on the computers without interruption or threat of detention. Just her and Peter, alone.

Now she had a mission and the courage to see it through.

• • •

"That's beautiful, Peter. Something new?" Peter's mom eased into the seat across from him to enjoy the gentle melody he played on the guitar. The bus rolled on toward New Mexico, and his brothers played video games in back.

"Yeah, I can't stop thinking about it." He held the guitar as if it were an extension of his body. His fingers manipulated the strings on his acoustic guitar and created a beautiful sound that drifted through the bus.

"That's always a good sign," she said.

Peter knew he possessed an innate talent for songwriting. When inspired, magic flowed and hits were born, but if he tried to force it, the songs flopped.

"You were gone a long time when we stopped in Rockville," his mother said.

"Yeah, great day for a walk." He strummed, working out a chord. "Did you know there are amazing rock formations farther in the park? One trail goes way back, and the temperature is, like, twenty degrees cooler, with ferns and moss growing everywhere." He stopped playing. "It's really cool."

"Is it your inspiration for this new song?" she asked with the hint of a smirk.

"Yeah, I guess." He resumed playing, the music calling him back.

"Did your new friend show it to you?"

His head snapped up, and his mom smiled.

"How'd you know?"

Her eyebrows rose, and her head tilted in suggestion.

"Adam." Peter frowned. "Of course."

"He can't help himself. He's just having fun. So tell me about this girl. What's her name?"

"Libby." Her beautiful face flashed in his mind.

"And?"

"And what?" He grinned, not about to offer more.

"Tell me about her. When my son disappears for two hours with a girl, I get to ask questions."

"Mom, I'll be eighteen soon, and then you don't get to ask anymore," he teased.

"That's what *you* think. Mothers have amazing powers of persuasion."

Peter laughed. "There's not much to tell. She lives in Rockville."

"Two hours and that's all you got? You want to tell me how you filled the rest of the time?"

Peter grinned. "Wouldn't you like to know." He strummed randomly.

"Peter." She pierced him with her sternest mom glare.

He laughed. "Okay, here's something juicy for you. She's never heard of Jamieson."

She looked doubtful. "I didn't think that was possible. Everyone knows about Jamieson, unless they live under a rock."

"I'm not gonna lie—I didn't think it was possible, either, but she seriously had no idea. It's pretty nice, really. When I told her about the band, she figured we play weddings and school dances."

"I see why you like her," she said.

"She's nice," he said, but offered nothing more and began to play again. His mom sat quietly and listened for a while.

"You know, on Saturday we'll be going back through that area."

Peter's heart leapt, but he played it cool. "Really? Do you think we can stop? I'd love to check out that area some more."

"I bet you would," she said.

"What?" He feigned innocence.

"I was just agreeing with you." His mother tried to control the grin on her face. "But, yes, I think we can stop."

Her cell phone rang. She stood to go answer it. "By

the way, what's the name of your new song?"

"'Angel Kisses,'" he answered.

• • •

The next day at school, Libby knocked on Miss Orman's open door, desperate to get her help.

"Hey, Libby, I haven't seen you for a while. How are you doing?" A half sandwich, a container of yogurt, and an apple sat on the desk near her keyboard.

"Good, thanks." Libby scanned the cramped office as she tried to get up the nerve to ask.

Miss Orman smiled at her knowingly. "Is there something in particular I can help you with?"

"Actually, yes." She eyed Miss Orman's PC and twisted the pendant she always wore. "I need to use a computer."

"Why don't you use the computer lab after school?"

"I can't do it before or after school. I ride the bus. And there's a class in the computer lab during my lunch."

"How about the computers in the library?" she asked.

"They're all busy." Libby offered her best pathetic, begging look.

Miss Orman seemed to consider her decision. "I take it this is very important to you?"

Libby nodded and held her breath. She needed to get back on the internet and check out some of the Peter Jamieson sites.

"Well, I suppose I could actually go to the lounge and eat lunch for a change, instead of making a mess out of my office." She glanced sideways at Libby. "Would right now be a good time?"

Libby nodded again, bringing a smile to Miss Orman's face.

"Tell you what, I'll make you a deal. You sell tickets for the Friday football game fan bus tomorrow during lunch, and I'll clear out right now."

"Done," Libby blurted. Even though she hated the idea of sitting alone at a table in the commons all through lunch, she'd agree to anything to get on Miss Orman's computer.

"All right, let me log off," she said as her fingers clicked on the keyboard to save and close files.

Libby's toe tapped in anticipation. Miss Orman grinned at her as she tidied the area around her keyboard and picked up her lunch items.

"I should be able to give you a good thirty minutes. Will that work?"

"Thank you. You have no idea how much this means to me."

"No problem. Have fun."

Once Miss Orman left, Libby nudged the door partly closed to discourage anyone from dropping in. She eased into the counselor's chair, enjoying the comfort.

This time, she didn't hesitate. She brought up the search engine, typed Peter's name, and hit ENTER. At the sight of his face on the screen, she squealed and stamped her feet.

"Yes, yes, yes!"

Immediately immersed in a world of Peter and the group called Jamieson, she went from one site to another, soaking up every word and photo. Jamieson was huge. They'd performed everywhere, including major sporting events, talk shows, and award shows. She couldn't believe she'd known nothing about them until now. Peter must think she lived under a rock, which was sort of true.

The time flew by so fast, she couldn't believe how soon Miss Orman returned. Libby's face must have shown disappointment, as she held the mouse about to click on a site with Jamieson's newest release.

"I guess I came back too soon."

"Has it really been a half hour?" She felt desperate to hear his voice again.

"It's been forty minutes. Didn't you hear the bell ring?"

"Oh my gosh, no." Her head jerked up to check the wall clock, confirming the late time. "I guess I better get going." She hated to do it, but she clicked the window closed, so Miss Orman wouldn't see what she'd been looking at: the official Jamieson site, with loads of pictures, music downloads, tour dates, blogs, and scheduled appearances. She could spend a day on it and never grow tired. How could she not have taken the time to hear their music?

"Did you find what you were looking for?"

Libby beamed as she stood and picked up her books.

"Yeah, thanks, I did. It was great." She felt a mix of euphoria from pouring over the details of Peter's life and regret at having to quit.

"Glad to help. You let me know if you need to get on again."

"I definitely will, thanks."

"Libby?"

"Yeah?" She turned back.

"Don't you think it would help if I gave you a late pass?"

"Oh yeah." Libby took the pink slip of paper and wandered out of the office toward her next class. All the photos of Peter and his brothers filled her head. Some were taken onstage, some from photo shoots, others greeting fans. Those were interesting. Lots of girls surrounded the three brothers, all with huge smiles, but she bet they never spent time alone with Peter just hanging out.

She needed to figure out how to get his music—and now—but she didn't have any money. This could take some creativity.

5

Peter waited backstage, a few days later, with his brothers. Despite the sound of the excited crowd, his mind wandered to his afternoon with Libby. He loved the time they spent together at Parfrey's Glen and hoped she'd be there Saturday. He didn't know why he felt this way; maybe because she didn't care who he was. But she didn't really know who he was, either. The thought made him smile. It also might be that Libby was his friend and no one else's. She had nothing to do with the band, the CD, or the tour.

"Hello, Earth to Peter." Garrett interrupted his thoughts. "You want to get your head in the game here?"

"What?" Peter scowled.

"You might want your earpiece."

Peter reached for his sound pack and found it absent. "Aw, man. I'll be right back." He rushed offstage to get it and was met halfway by a panicked sound tech who quickly hooked him up.

"You've got it bad, man!" Garrett yelled after him. "Real bad!"

Once back in place and ready, Peter waited for their intro. The crowd in the arena went wild. The combined energy built to epic levels. The backup band was positioned at the rear of the stage. Garrett waited stage left, bass guitar in hand. Adam mirrored him on stage right, with Peter anchored in the center. His blood rushed in anticipation as their moment grew near. God, he loved this.

The music built in a huge crescendo, spotlights roamed the arena, and fog rolled onto the stage. The trio of brothers nodded to one another, in sync and ready to rock. Adam went first, a spotlight illuminating him; he grinned and hit the opening chord; the crowd went into a frenzy. Moments later, Garrett appeared, guitar in hand. The audience cheered as he joined Adam in musical power. Finally, Peter stepped into the lights, and the crowd went ballistic.

Peter loved this part of the night. After a long afternoon of rehearsal, sound checks, and final warm-ups, it was time for the payoff. He gave his signature welcome to the audience, nodding in several directions, each time eliciting more cheers. He stepped up to his mic stand and held it in anticipation. His body pulsed to the beat as he waited for his entrance. He gazed out over the vast crowd, filled with confidence and power.

The audience rocked to the music. Eager and excited, they became putty in his hands. The moment came. The guitars hit his key, the drum and cymbals crashed, and the lights exploded in color. In that same instant, Peter swung the mic stand and nailed his opening note, his body taut with strength and energy. His pure voice rose above the instruments; his lyrics hit the back wall. He owned the stage. All eyes were on him. The night was young, and he was ready to rock.

Song after song, the three moved with a synchronicity only possible among brothers. They worked off each other's signals, and moved from individual highlights and solos to unison movement. At times, they delivered their carefully crafted harmonies, singing together at one mic, their heads inches apart. They exchanged silent communication. When they were onstage, they displayed complete and utter harmony of movement, thought, and talent. They hummed with energy.

While Garrett and Adam awed with their expert guitar stylings, Peter ramped things up with stage moves, mic tricks, and vocals. He mesmerized the audience.

Perspiration glistened over his body. His mop of hair dripped with sweat. He whipped it to the side as he belted each note. He left every ounce of energy onstage; he held nothing back and the audience knew it. Peter peered out over the thousands of fans and watched as the lights illuminated different areas of the audience that the three brothers, Jamieson, held in a spell. The experience of sharing the music he created never failed to intoxicate him.

• • •

That Friday, Libby sank low in her folding chair and buried her head in a copy of *The Great Gatsby*. At least the book helped her appear a little less obvious as she sold tickets among the riotous noise of the commons area.

True to her word, Miss Orman expected her to sell bus tickets to the away football game that night. Some cheerleader should be stuck at the table, not her.

She'd sold a dozen or so tickets, but most of the students ignored her. Libby had become invisible to them months earlier. Of course, she didn't help the situation any by trying to fit in. When she started school in Rockville, her heart overflowed with grief and thoughts of her mom and her sister, Sarah. Her withdrawn personality mistakenly convinced the kids she was a loner, but even the loners had found her eerily withdrawn. Libby's only problem was that she suffered terrible grief. But everything changed the day Peter walked into her life. Now all she could concentrate on was him and how unbelievable it was that he actually wanted to see her again.

Since checking Peter out on the internet, she'd thought of nothing else. When they talked at Parfrey's Glen, she thought he'd exaggerated the popularity of their band. In reality, he'd understated it.

She couldn't imagine why he wanted to see her on Saturday, but she wasn't going to second-guess his sanity. She could barely wait to lay eyes on him again and make sure she didn't dream up the whole thing. The hour crept by so slowly, she wanted to scream.

If only she could figure out a way to get his music, then she could hear his voice and pretend he was near. She needed a connection to Peter, some way to get a little closer. But she had no money and no way to download music to her iPod. If she could just get her hands on a CD, but there was no way to go to a store outside of school hours, let alone pay for it.

Aunt Marge insisted Libby spend all her time studying or at Parfrey's Glen for the fresh air. She was paranoid Libby might do something remotely normal like get a job, have friends over, or, God forbid, go on a date. Libby suspected her aunt possessed other motives, but it never bothered her until now. She was used to her aunt's bizarre and strict behavior. Libby had never questioned her authority; she always gave in.

A group of freshman girls walked up and bought tickets.

"Thanks," their chirpy little voices said.

"Yup," Libby mumbled as they walked away.

Libby picked up the crinkled bills and smoothed them. Out of boredom she arranged them in the same direction. As she flipped the bills around, it dawned on her that she held enough money to buy Peter's CD. Her heart stopped for a moment.

Stealing is wrong.

She placed the bills in the metal cash box and closed it. She would not do it. She'd find another way.

Her determination wavered. The money would solve her problem so fast. No one would miss a few dollars. In the grand scheme of things, seventeen dollars was nothing.

Never in her life had Libby taken anything from anyone, but this was different. Her aunt only gave her enough money for lunch, nothing more. If Libby needed clothing, her aunt drove her to the thrift store to pick out a couple items. It humiliated Libby to buy other people's castoffs, but she wasn't allowed to get a job, and she didn't have access to money. Now that she thought about it, she realized how much Aunt Marge controlled her life and she didn't like the taste of it. Not at all.

The only way she could get Peter's CD was to be creative. Taking this money qualified.

She peered around the crowded commons area. No one seemed to notice her or the tempting cash box. She chewed on her lip and tapped her toe against the table leg. After a minute or so, she reached forward and opened the lid. Her pulse raced. She grabbed a couple five-dollar bills and a handful of ones.

She pulled her hand out, folded the bills, and slid them into her back pocket. She kept her head down. If she didn't look at anyone, they wouldn't look at her. She sat tapping her foot back and forth, counting the final minutes until the bell. At last it rang and her ticket-selling session ended.

Libby grabbed her books and the cash box and walked to the front office. She quickly dropped off the box with the old secretary and left, her head held low in shame. The stolen money burned in her back pocket like a hot coal.

Without hesitating, she went straight to her locker, stuffed her books inside, and grabbed her coat. She swallowed down her guilt. She would not let her conscience get in the way. As the remaining students straggled to their next class, Libby strode out the school doors.

6

Twenty minutes later, Libby's worn-out shoes padded through the discount store. She wanted to go unnoticed, but the bright store lights shone down, revealing her presence. Guilt hung on her shoulders like a heavy chain.

She found the entertainment section filled with electronics, video games, and DVDs. She searched one aisle and then another. Nothing. Panic crept over her. She had little time to return to school and catch her bus.

"Can I help you?" A middle-aged man with a big belly held a scanning device in his hand and waited for her response.

"Uh, yes," she whispered, then cleared her throat and spoke louder. "I was wondering where you keep the CDs?"

"Down here on the end," he replied, turning and walking down the aisle. She trailed after him. Did he wonder why a high school kid was in the store during the middle of the afternoon?

He turned the corner. "Country and show tunes are on this side, rock and jazz on the other, new releases are on the aisle end. Is there anything particular you're looking for?"

"Jamieson?" she answered, quieter than she meant to.

"Their display is on the end. You can't miss it." To Libby's relief, he turned and went in the opposite direction.

Libby tried not to rush as she moved to the end of the aisle. There stood a six-foot-tall cutout photo of a smiling Peter, Garrett, and Adam, advertising their latest album. Libby stood back in awe. Her hand reached out and touched the glossy cardboard imitation of Peter. The huge display dominated space next to a wall of Jamieson CDs, every copy featuring Peter Jamieson smiling back at her.

Never in her wildest thoughts did she imagine he was so famous. He'd given none of it away when they'd been together. She wanted to scream with joy. She picked up a plastic-encased CD; his handsome face looked exactly as she remembered. She grinned back at him, then cradled the coveted music. The risk of cutting classes and coming all this way was worth whatever punishment Aunt Marge might dish out.

When Libby checked out, her hands shook as she passed the stolen bills to the checker. For a split instant, she thought of how disappointed her mom would have been about her stealing, but Libby wiped the thought away. She walked out of the store and looked in both directions to be sure no one watched. She darted around the side of the store and pulled her prize from the bag. She ripped the packaging off as quickly as she could with her still-shaking hands. Then the clear tape wouldn't let her by. She picked at it, then used a nail file to lift the edge. Finally, she won the battle. Inside the case lay a perfect, untouched CD, and a glossy booklet containing lyrics and more pictures of Peter and his brothers.

Her heart sang and her eyes watered with giddy excitement. It belonged to her! After a couple minutes of idol worship, she reluctantly tucked it back in the bag and into her small pack. She rushed back to school, afraid she would miss the afternoon bus home or get caught walking up to school as everyone else left.

She made it back to Aunt Marge's without a hitch. As soon as she got there, Libby snuck up to her room. She placed a chair against the door in case her aunt came up. The rest of the afternoon and that night she pored over the glossy booklet cover to cover, while listening to the CD through earbuds on an old portable CD player. She recognized Peter's amazing voice in every song and still couldn't believe she'd spent a sunny afternoon talking to him just days before. More than ever she wished Sarah were here to share her excitement.

Late in the night, Libby drifted off with the glorious

sound of Peter's voice lulling her to sleep. There were no bad dreams that night.

• • •

"Dad, come on. It's not even out of the way."

Peter continued to push. He refused to back down. He told Libby he'd be there today and he planned to keep his word. Garrett and Adam looked on, eager to see who would win the power struggle. Why couldn't anything in his life be private?

"We're already behind schedule. We've got production meetings on the video shoot for tomorrow, you boys have interviews and wardrobe fittings, plus I've got some tour issues to iron out," he said from the small table at the front of the bus. Today they had their hired driver, as they always did for longer trips.

Dad could be immovable at times. He always wanted life to be neat and tidy like his pleated pants.

"Just because this isn't important to you, doesn't mean it's not important to me," Peter said. "I gave my word. That should be worth something." He stood his ground, waiting for the response he wanted. The only way to get through to his dad was to out-logic him.

"I don't think it's a good idea to start letting girls influence your life. You've got plenty of girls chasing after you on tour. What's so different about this one?"

"That's the point; she *is* different. She's not like all

the other screaming fools. She's interesting and fun, and she doesn't care about all the band stuff. She'd never even heard of Jamieson before I told her."

"I thought everyone on the planet knew us," Adam piped up from the couch as he clicked through the camera's stored photos.

Peter turned and fixed his little brother with a stare.

"Peter, it's pouring rain out there. If this girl has any sense, she won't be standing in this deluge waiting for you. And if she is, well, that's another issue," his dad said.

Peter turned to his mother. "Mom, please, ya gotta help me out here."

"You know, Jett," his mother said in that soothing "I'm gonna get my way" tone, "we've always encouraged the boys to have lives outside of their music."

"I was talking about playing soccer, not chasing girls."

Peter's eyes darted from one parent to the other as if watching a tennis match. He didn't dare say a word to distract them.

"What could it hurt?" she added.

"All right, but no more than an hour. I'm not sitting around in the rain waiting for Romeo here."

Peter and his mom smiled.

"We'll go grab a quick lunch while Peter checks to see if . . ." She turned to Peter. "What is her name?"

"Libby."

"Yes, that's right, Libby. If Libby is there."

His father grunted his assent.

"Thank you," Peter mouthed to his mom.

She responded with a smile and a pat on his arm.

"Score," he said under his breath, pumping his fist.

7

The instant the door opened, Peter flew out of the bus, ignoring the steady rain. His footsteps sank into the soggy grass as he ran across the clearing and past the large oak where he had first met Libby. He made his way down the muddy path, which led him closer to the stream. The slick ground slowed his progress. *Please let her be here.*

The rain came down in a constant stream, muffling sounds in the glen. Peter rounded a bend and spotted Libby standing in the center of the large rock that hung over the stream. He paused and smiled. She grinned back. She wore a dark green Windbreaker and jeans. One hand was tucked into her coat pocket, the other held a huge, blue-and-white faded umbrella. Its enormity dwarfed her. She looked like a cute little garden gnome who'd been left out in the rain.

Peter closed the distance in seconds. "You're here!"

"So are you." She smiled, her hair damp. Peter noticed several gaping holes in the umbrella, causing a constant flow of water onto her.

"I was so worried you wouldn't be here, with the rain and all. Have you been waiting long?" He wanted to reach out and hug her, but didn't quite know how to make it happen.

"No, not long at all." A shiver racked her body.

"Liar. Your lips are turning blue." Peter's eyes settled on her trembling mouth.

"You're getting soaked. Come stand under the umbrella." She lifted it enough to clear his height. In the process of tipping the umbrella, a sheet of cold water swooshed off the back and splashed their legs as it hit the rock.

"Oops, sorry," she said with a giggle.

Peter crowded close under the umbrella. He gazed down at her smiling face. Raindrops clung to her eyelashes.

"What do you say we go somewhere we won't get pummeled by rain?" He took the umbrella from Libby and wrapped his arm around her small frame. They moved off the rock and climbed to an area near the wall. Trees reached over the glen, blocking some of the rain. The constant downfall now sounded like a pitter-patter.

Peter reached for her hand and held the oversized umbrella with his other. "Jeez, your hand is freezing."

"I'm not gonna lie, it was really cold out here, but I didn't want to stand you up." Her cheeks were chafed red from the cold. "So I hope you plan on making it worth my while." She teased him with a sly look.

"Now that you mention it, I did have something in mind."

Libby's eyes widened.

"I have something for you." He had moved heaven and earth to pull this together.

"You do?" Her eyes glittered in surprise.

"Yup. Close your eyes and hold out your hands." He couldn't wait to see what she thought. Libby obeyed. Her dark eyelashes lay against her rosy cheeks. His heart beat in anticipation. He reached into his jacket pocket and pulled out a white plastic bag, then glanced up. Her closed eyes changed to little slits.

"Hey, stop peeking!"

Libby squeezed her eyes closed and laughed. She held out her hands and waited. Peter pulled the slim item out of the bag and placed it in her hands.

"Okay, look."

She peered at the shiny device and then back at him in disbelief. "You gave me a cell phone?" She stared at the gift. "You gave me a cell phone!" This time she yelled it.

"It seemed like a good idea. You didn't have a phone number to give me, and I really missed you. It's gonna get harder to see you. I thought this way we could stay in touch and actually talk whenever we want."

She closed her hand around the precious phone and turned pensive.

"Is something wrong?"

"I don't know if I should accept this." She gazed up at him. He couldn't believe this. He needed her to take the phone.

"We barely know each other, and, well . . ." Mischief lit her face, and he wondered what she was up to. "We've never even kissed."

Peter paused and took a good look at her. He'd been wondering how to sneak a kiss.

He tossed the umbrella aside and pulled her close. He let his fingers tangle in her wet hair and lowered his mouth to hers. He kissed her long, taking his sweet time. Cold rain trickled down his neck as he savored each moment. Startled at first, Libby now returned his kiss. He enjoyed the touch of her tender lips.

He slowly pulled away. "Now can you take the phone?" His forehead rested against hers.

"Yeah, I think so," she answered with a breathy voice and a sly smile.

"I'd better be sure." Empowered by their perfect chemistry, he leaned in for more. Her body melted against him. He wrapped his other arm around her and pulled her close.

"Wow," she whispered, her eyes dark and smoky.

"Haven't you ever been kissed before?" His eyes searched hers.

"Not like that."

"Good." Nothing like kissing a girl senseless to boost his confidence. "I think I'll just stay here all day. The rain's not so bad." He caressed her damp cheek with his thumb.

"I'd like that." She leaned her head back against the rock wall, gazing contently up into his eyes.

"The tour is overrated anyway," he said.

Libby leaned into him. Everything about her brought Peter alive. His life was great, a dream come true; he had nothing to complain about. But this simple girl turned everything upside down. He couldn't get enough. He wanted to sneak her onto the bus and take her with him.

They parted, breathless and secure in each other's arms.

Peter's phone suddenly rang. His family was back. "I should have sent them to Iowa for lunch."

"You can't leave me now." She sighed from her spot in Peter's arms.

"What are we going to do?"

They had opened a new door and complicated their lives. Neither wanted to walk away.

"We're going to talk as often as possible and text in between," he said, hoping to reassure her that this was only the beginning.

"Okay, but when will I see you again?" she asked, the angst clear in her eyes.

"I don't know. We're leaving the Midwest for a while." Not knowing worried him, too. "But that isn't going to stop us from being together. I'll figure something out. I promise."

He meant it with every fiber of his being. They barely knew each other, but they would soon. He refused to let her go. The connection they shared couldn't be denied.

Libby nodded, her trust in him absolute. His phone played music again.

"You're ringing."

"They can wait. I'm with them all the time."

He lowered his lips to hers once more, feeling neither the cold nor the rain.

• • •

Peter jogged through the steady rain, his heart bursting with joy. The silver bus waited, surrounded by a thick fog.

He hammered on the door twice. It opened smoothly. He returned to the other part of his life, energized and empowered. He could conquer the world.

"Peter, where's Libby?" his mother asked.

He pushed the hood of his jacket back and shook his head like a dog, spraying water on everyone around him.

"Dude, grab a towel, would ya?" Adam blocked his face with his arm.

"She didn't want a ride. She's not far from home and wanted to walk."

His parents exchanged concerned glances.

"She's really shy, that's all."

"Apparently, not too shy," Adam said, noticing Peter's euphoric mood.

Peter shrugged, a smug grin on his face. He moved to the back of the bus, high-fiving Garrett as he passed.

"Oh yeah, little brother," Garrett said.

"We brought you a burger," his mother called.

"Not hungry." He plopped onto the couch, popped in his earphones, and lost himself in thoughts of Libby.

• • •

A half hour later, Libby's sopping-wet jeans lay in a pile on the floor along with her waterlogged shoes and dripping socks. She sat in the middle of her bed with her new phone and ran her hands over it when a familiar Jamieson tune played.

Startled, she dropped the phone, then fumbled with the screen until she heard laughter sound from the tiny unit.

She picked it up. "Hello?"

"Hey there." Peter's magical voice sounded close.

"Peter!"

"Your voice is music to my ears," Peter answered.

Libby felt warm and tingly down to her cold feet. "I can't believe you gave me a phone."

"Well, I had to do something. I couldn't quit the tour and hide in the woods every day, waiting for you. My dad would have blown a gasket. I figured this would be a good compromise."

"Works for me."

"Whatcha doing?" he asked.

"Sitting on my bed looking at all this stuff that goes with the phone. I just got here a few minutes ago."

"Perfect timing. You'll have to be sure to put it on mute when you're at school."

"I've decided to quit school so I can talk to you all day."

"No, you won't. You need to study, get smart, and graduate."

She couldn't stop grinning. This was almost like having him there with her. "Never fear. I'm only a few credits from finishing."

"Are you a senior?"

"No, I'm a junior, but I have enough credits to graduate at the end of the semester."

"How'd you manage that? I just finished last spring, and I swore it would kill me. I hated homework. It kept me from writing songs."

"I spend a lot of time studying. I've had a lot of time on my hands, so I just loaded up on extra classes and took summer courses." Studying had been her savior. Losing herself in books made the rest of the world go away. You don't think about how much you miss your family when you're deep into advanced biology or calculus.

"So you're a brainiac?"

"Maybe," she replied with a smile. "Does that bother you?"

"Heck, no. Maybe some of your smarts will rub off on me."

She laughed. "So, where are you? What are you doing?"

"We're headed south, to Texas, and I'm sitting in my bunk talking to this really cool girl I know."

Libby hugged herself. "Texas is far. How long till you get there?"

"I think it's about sixteen hours to Dallas, so I have a lot of time to talk."

"I can handle that, but I'm going to have to plug in the phone or we'll drain the battery on the first time out."

She talked to him late into the night about anything and everything. She accidentally cut him off twice. It felt like they'd known each other forever.

Peter's family interrupted off and on throughout their marathon conversation. Somewhere around two thirty in the morning, their energy began to wane, so they agreed to hang up and begin again the next day. They would try texting throughout the day, since she had school.

Libby fell asleep with the phone snuggled up against her, a symbol of the soul mate she'd found.

• • •

"Libby, you're wanted in the office." Ms. Dorsett, her American Literature teacher, held a pink slip of paper.

Libby closed the heavy textbook and grabbed her papers. She'd never been called to the office before and couldn't imagine why it happened today. As she walked through the vacant halls, her mind searched for a reason. Then it hit her.

Dad!

He said he'd be back for her. When he dropped her off last year, he said it was only for a couple of weeks, but it turned into over a year. Finally, she could escape Rockville. She hurried the remainder of the distance. Wait until he heard about Peter. Libby burst through the office doors, searching for her father's kind face. He had been a pillar of strength before the accident broke him.

The gray-haired secretary glanced up from her work. "I'll be right with you, dear."

Libby's heart beat in anticipation. She went around the corner and peeked into Miss Orman's office. No Dad enjoying a nice visit with the counselor while he waited for her. Miss Orman glanced up from a call, her smile strained.

Libby returned to the main office and sighed.

"Principal Harried will see you now," the elderly secretary said.

Was her dad in with the principal? Something didn't feel right. She moved past the counter and down the short hall to the open door of the principal's office. She paused, unsure if she should knock or walk right in.

"Ah, Miss Sawyer, please come in and take a seat. Close the door behind you."

As Libby shut the heavy door with a solid *click* and took a seat in a worn chair facing the principal's desk, dread pressed in. Please don't let something have happened to her dad. She couldn't bear it.

Principal Harried closed the folder in front of him and removed his glasses from his pointy nose; his bulging eyes reminded her of a rodent's. The kids called him Rat.

"It appears we have a problem." He leaned back in his chair and narrowed his eyes, delaying the news.

Libby gripped her hands. Her mouth went dry as words eluded her.

"Last Friday you sold bus tickets for the away football game. Is that correct?" His eyes pierced hers.

Oh crap.

The heat of guilt climbed her neck. "Yes, sir." She swallowed.

"One of the women working in the lunch line saw you take money from the cash box and pocket it. Is that correct?" He spoke slowly and quietly.

More than anything, she wanted to lie. The only time in her life she'd ever taken anything, and now she was caught. Panic hit. *Deny it. Lie.* She could taste the words on the tip of her tongue. She wasn't a bad person; she just needed the money.

"Before you answer, I want you to know that the same cash box came up short seventeen dollars." He tapped his finger against his temple; he had her cornered.

"Yes, sir." She crossed her arms, hugging herself tight.

"What was that?" Principal Rat asked.

"Yes, sir. I took the money." Libby's head hung low. No wonder she always followed the rules; breaking them and getting caught sucked.

"Would you like to explain yourself?" He crossed his arms, his voice tight.

"No, sir," she mumbled.

"Excuse me?" Apparently, he wasn't used to hearing no.

"No, sir, I wouldn't like to explain." If she confessed about her CD, he'd probably take it away.

"I see." He rubbed the bridge of his nose. "Well, young lady, we have zero tolerance for stealing in this school. Let me spell this out so you understand the full consequence of your actions. You will serve an in-school detention, you will return the money, and your guardian will be notified."

"Please don't call her," Libby interrupted in a full panic. "I'm really sorry. I didn't plan to do it. I'll do whatever detention you want, but please don't call her."

"We have strict policies in this school, and perhaps this will help deter you from stealing again. I've already called her. You can expect to be disciplined at home as well."

Why did life always have to be so complicated? Could nothing ever go her way? How could she go home and face her aunt?

"Miss Orman will oversee your detention, and you can return the money to Mrs. Keller at the front desk."

"I don't have it anymore. I spent it."

He leaned back in his chair again, glanced at her file, and sighed a deep breath, clearly annoyed. "I assume that would explain your unexcused absence Friday afternoon."

She nodded.

"Well, we'll be sure to find a way for you to work the money off. Let this be a strong message to you. If this should happen again, you will be looking at a suspension. You may go."

8

Entering the gloomy farmhouse felt like walking into a prison. Libby always worked hard to avoid confrontations with Aunt Marge. The woman had a warped sense of right and wrong, and Libby could never figure out where her thinking came from. Thank God for Peter and her new phone. She texted him throughout the day and on the bus ride home; it made this crummy day tolerable. His humor gave her the courage to face Aunt Marge.

Libby peeked into the living room, which was empty, except for her aunt's clutter of beer cans and old copies of the *National Enquirer*. As quietly as possible, she stepped into the kitchen, then startled.

Aunt Marge closed the fridge and popped open a beer as she spotted Libby. Her frizzy, gray hair stuck out around her wrinkled face.

"Well, well, well. The little criminal shows her face."

Libby fixed her gaze at the floor, hoping to prevent a fight, then slunk over to the stairs. The best solution was to disappear to her room.

"Where do you think you're going? Get back here. Your principal thinks we need to have a talk." She folded her arms across her faded shirt.

Libby lowered her backpack to the floor and returned to the kitchen doorway.

"So what do you have to say for yourself?" Aunt Marge asked with the voice of an evil witch.

Libby knew a trick question when she heard it. No matter what she said, it wouldn't change the temperature of the hot water she was in.

"Speak up. Don't play your shy game with me, I know better." Aunt Marge leaned against the counter, which was cluttered with piles of dirty dishes and stacks of junk mail, sales flyers, and unpaid bills.

"I'm sorry."

What more could she say? If she had money, she wouldn't need to steal. Her parents would have given her an allowance, or at least let her get a job and earn her own money.

"Sorry? Do you really think you can make this go away with a simple sorry? Ha!" she spat. "That arrogant principal pulled me away from my work to preach about the value of integrity and discipline. He seems to think I haven't been firm enough with you." She glared resentfully at Libby.

Libby stood silent, waiting for the storm to hit full force. And what work could Aunt Marge possibly be pulled away from?

"So what are we gonna do about this?" Aunt Marge took a drag of her beer; the smell of hops hung in the air. "Your stealing shows your need for attention. What was so important you needed money for?"

Libby couldn't tell her about the Jamieson CD; she'd take it away or destroy it. The CD belonged to her, regardless of how she got it. What could she say? Her mind darted for something, anything to explain it.

"I bought perfume," she blurted. "From the drugstore." Hopefully, that would appease her.

Aunt Marge's eyes narrowed. "Perfume, what for?"

"I just wanted to smell good. I always smell like smoke."

Her aunt's lip curled in distaste. "Is that so? You saying it stinks in here?"

Libby watched her aunt peer around the kitchen as if seeing it for the first time. Piles of dirty clothes stank in a corner, the garbage can overflowed with beer cans, and the kitchen table strained under more junk and clutter.

"Well, we can't have Your Royal Highness unhappy. Tell you what. Since you're so upset about the way you smell, this is the perfect time for you to clean up this place." A cruel smile appeared on her thin lips.

"But I have homework." It would take hours, maybe days, to clean this disaster. She needed to get back to Peter.

"You can start with the kitchen today, and we'll have you work your way through the house, a new room every day. You'll smell fresh and clean like lemon Pledge when you're done."

"But . . ." Libby interrupted.

"Uh-uh-uh." Her aunt pointed a tobacco-stained finger at her. Her voice crooned innocence, but darkness threatened below the surface. "You are not in a position to argue. I do not *ever* want to hear the voice of your principal again. You have a lot of work to do." She tilted her beer can and poured it onto the kitchen floor. "It's a real mess in here." Aunt Marge sneered as she trailed out of the kitchen letting the remainder of her beer trickle throughout the house as she went.

• • •

Libby was plotting the fifty ways she'd get back at her aunt.

But despite Libby's anger, she dove into her punishment with fervor, beginning with the mountain of dirty dishes and utensils. It took forever, since dried food cemented itself to the surface of every item. After a few hours, the room began to resemble a normal kitchen, except the table still overflowed with papers. It surprised Libby, the pride she felt cleaning up the pigsty. She dragged the trash bin to the table and took a seat where she began to sort through the piles. She tossed newspapers and junk mail, discovered a long-forgotten loaf of bread growing penicillin for anyone brave enough to touch it. She scooped the bread into the trash bag with a newspaper.

She grabbed an empty envelope, but something about it caught her eye. She paused and stared down at the familiar handwriting. Her heart raced as she reached in and retrieved it.

Her name was printed on the envelope in her father's neat penmanship.

Libby's breath caught in her throat. He hadn't forgotten her. She looked inside, but the envelope was empty. She scanned the messy table for the letter, then returned to the envelope. The postmark read MAY 16, ATLANTA, GEORGIA.

Atlanta? Why was he in Atlanta? Thoughts rushed through her mind. Did he have a new job there? Was he coming to get her soon?

Libby set the precious envelope aside and turned back to the mountain of trash on the table before her. She rifled through it, tossing odd items to the floor, heedless of the new mess she created. Where was the letter? Her urgency grew as her fingers touched item after item.

Hidden under a plate of fossilized pizza, Libby discovered another envelope. Her heart soared as she pulled out the single sheet and read.

Dear Libby,

I hope this letter finds you happy in Rockville, enjoying the carefree days of high school. I'm sorry I'm not there for you, but losing your mother and Sarah has sent me to a painful place I don't know how to escape.

The last months I've driven the back roads of the South, trying to make sense of all that has happened. One day we had it all, and the next it was gone. No one ever taught me how to survive such loss. Part of me wishes to see you again, but the other part knows that every time I look at you, I will see your mother and sister looking back. It breaks my heart. Please forgive your old man for his weakness.

Here are a few dollars. Go out with your friends and catch a movie or buy something nice. God knows you deserve better.

Dad

Tears rolled down her cheeks. She traced his signature with her finger. Touching the ink was the closest she could get to him. Didn't he want her anymore? Libby picked up the envelope and flipped it over. The faded postmark read JUNE 29, TATUM, NEW MEXICO. Now it was October. He had abandoned her at Aunt Marge's. Didn't he know how much she needed him?

She wiped away the tears with her sleeve. Crying wouldn't help anything. She returned to the remaining mess on the table, searching for more correspondence, but discovered nothing. Her heart felt empty and lonely as she sat with two envelopes and a sad letter. Loneliness settled around her.

The phone vibrated in her back pocket, forcing her thoughts back to the present. Peter. A small smile lit her face. She reached for the phone and read the text.

Concert's over, can you talk?

Her fingers fumbled over the screen of her new toy.

No, soon. I'll call you.

She returned the phone to the safety of her pocket. Before she talked to Peter, there was something she needed to do.

Libby walked into the darkened living room, letter in hand. Things were about to change. Her aunt had some questions to answer, and Libby refused to be bullied anymore. Aunt Marge snored lightly in her chair, and QVC droned in the background. How did one wake a sleeping monster?

Libby turned off the TV and flipped on a light, illuminating the harsh room.

Her aunt sputtered. "What? Who's there?"

Libby waited, patient. Aunt Marge shook off her sleep and sat up straighter, her eyes narrow slits of suspicion.

"What's your problem now? Got that kitchen clean?"

"Why didn't you tell me?"

"Tell you what?"

"About this?" She held out the letter, far enough so her aunt could see it, but not take it. The woman would never touch Libby's letter again.

Realization washed across her aunt's face. Her posture tensed for a split second and then relaxed. "Oh, that." She waved her hand, then reached for a pack of cigarettes.

"This letter belongs to me. Why didn't you give it to me?"

"I guess I forgot." She placed a cigarette in her mouth and lit it.

"Where is the other letter? And where is the money he sent?" Libby glared at her, willing to fight this to the end. Aunt Marge was keeping her from her dad.

"First off, this is my house, not yours. Anything in it belongs to me, and I'll do what I want with it." She took a long drag on the cigarette. "Secondly, your father owes me far more than the paltry money he adds to his letters. Fifty dollars a month doesn't begin to pay for your food, let alone all the other things you need." She blew the smoke into the air between them.

"Once a month! He's written every month?" Libby couldn't believe it. She had missed him so much and here he'd been writing regularly. "Where are the letters? They belong to me. I want them. Now!" She stepped closer, her hands on her hips in a vain attempt to appear threatening.

"They're gone. Burned out back," she answered, unfazed. "You should thank me, too. All he did was drivel on about how sad he is. Trust me, you don't need his ramblings. When you got here, you were a shy mousy little thing afraid of your own shadow. Look at you now! Not only are you standing up for yourself, you're shoplifting."

She tipped the ash of her cigarette into an overflowing ashtray. "You're growing a backbone. It's enough to make your auntie proud, but I can't be having you getting caught. That will not do."

"I didn't shoplift," Libby stated through clenched teeth.

"Yeah, whatever. You stole the cash, that's all that matters."

"And if I had the money my dad sent, I would have never lowered myself to that level."

"Never say never. You'd be surprised at how that can come back to bite you in the ass."

"You don't know anything about me, so don't pretend you do. The next time my father writes, I expect to get the letter. Unopened." God, she hated this woman.

"You'd better learn to watch your mouth, or I'll be doing it for you. Oh, and I wouldn't go expecting anything soon. He hasn't written in a few months. He's probably moved on and forgotten you. It's just you and me now, two peas in a pod." A tiny bug crawled across the arm of her chair. Aunt

Marge grabbed a nearby newspaper and squashed it.

Libby wanted to reach out and slap the woman, but knew she never could. With lack of a good comeback, she turned on her heel and stomped upstairs. She needed privacy, away from this horrible woman who seemed to enjoy Libby's pain. Plus, Peter was waiting for her call. Talking to him would instantly take her mind off her troubles and her aunt's betrayal. She slammed her door for effect.

9

After two weeks of late-night whispering and daily texting, Peter finally met up with Libby at Parfrey's Glen for a full day together.

"I'd sure love to see you perform," Libby said as they meandered through the woods, hand in hand.

"You want to come to a concert?" Peter acted surprised.

"Of course I do! But that's not going to happen. Not unless you're playing Rockville High School's homecoming dance."

"Hmm, that's a good idea. I've always wanted to go to homecoming; plus, I could call you out in front of everyone and declare my love." He pulled her close.

Peter said he loved her! Sort of. Her face turned a predictable shade of pink. She was speechless.

"What? I've discovered how to keep you quiet for a change?" Peter grinned, enjoying her embarrassment.

Libby smacked him lightly on the arm, then rested her head on his shoulder. "I'm not saying a thing." But inside she glowed.

"So the girl wants a performance. Hmm. I can't afford to have an unhappy fan. I believe this calls for an impromptu show."

He led her to a clearing surrounded by tall pines. "Miss, here is your front-row seat. The concert will begin in just a moment." Peter walked a good twenty feet away and hid behind a clump of brush.

"No peeking. This is backstage and strictly off-limits to general ticket holders."

Libby turned her head away and held back a smile.

"Ladies and gentlemen," he roared in a mock announcer's voice. "I mean, girl in the front row sitting on the ground."

Libby threw a pinecone at him.

"Hey, I haven't started yet! You can't boo until I do something."

She leaned back on her hands. She couldn't wait to see what he did next.

"Girl in the front row, I present to you . . . the Jamieson brothers. I mean, Peter Jamieson."

He sauntered out from behind the brush making faux roaring noises. "The crowd goes wild for Jamieson. *Rrrrrr.*" He walked to center stage, in front of a bush, and picked up a stick for a microphone.

"Jamieson has entered the building." He raised his hands toward the sky and let loose another crowd roar.

"The two-million-megawatt lighting system kicks up. Spotlights search the arena for the star. Lasers ripple through the air. Fog rises around the stage. The intro music builds." Peter motioned dramatically to the trees and bushes around them as if this were the real deal.

"The cheers in the arena are deafening!" He waved his hands in the air again, making another *rrr* sound.

Libby laughed. Peter stepped forward onto his imaginary stage.

"The star! The legend! Feast your eyes on the world's most talented singer, PETER JAMIESON!" He roared into the open expanse of nature.

"Girls are fainting at the mere mention of his name," he whispered to the side.

Libby watched as Peter paced his mock stage, setting the scene.

"First starts the tinkling of piano keys; the lights pick up the beat." His fingers played the imaginary piano and then motioned at pretend lights.

"Bass guitarist, Garrett, sadly, a sub-par performer, enters the mix."

She giggled.

"Next, lead guitarist, adolescent voyeur, Adam, adds his soulful sound. And then . . ." Peter held the fake microphone like a pro and started to sing.

Peter's pure voice rang through the woods. Libby watched, so overwhelmed by his talent that the words didn't register. All she could do was watch his moves, his stance, and listen to his amazing voice. Libby sat dumbstruck in the pine needles and leaves.

"Here's where the drums take the beat, *ch ch cha, ch ch cha, ch ch cha.*" He played the imaginary drum. "The guitars come in, *tinka ting, tinka ting,* and Peter Jamieson fades to the back, giving his mediocre brothers a chance to shine." He rewarded her with a wink.

"And then, the melody takes back the night." He stood atop an old, fallen log and sang, his entire body creating the percussion that went unheard. It captivated Libby and transported her to the concert hall.

"Then, to seal the deal, the Boy Wonder awes the audience with his world-class flying eagle." Peter jumped high into the air above her, reached out, and touched his toes.

Libby's eyes followed him like an awestruck fan.

He landed and picked up the song again, gesturing the percussion and guitar licks as he went.

Peter's talent far exceeded her wildest imagination. He was an incredibly gifted performer, and she'd never understood it until now. Sure, he was well-known, but it never affected her. Time and distance was their barrier, nothing else. His cute, cocky performance revealed only a small hint of the talent flowing just beneath the surface. His voice held power and confidence and moved her to tears.

"Hey, I'm ready for the big finish." Peter posed, feet set wide apart, his fake mic replaced with a long walking stick. He gripped the mock mic stand firmly and leaned to the side, while his body kept the beat.

He looked up from his rocker pose. "What's wrong?"

Libby covered her mouth with her hand.

Peter rushed over and squatted before her. "What's the matter? Was I that bad?"

"That's not funny." She pushed out at him, as tears welled in her eyes.

"I'm sorry. Garrett can't help playing so bad."

His joke hit the mark, and she laughed, then took a deep breath. "I didn't realize"—she shook her head—"that you're so good." She couldn't help but feel devastated. Her life was so tiny and unimportant and his was over-the-top huge. Peter didn't belong with her. He should be with a famous model or actress.

He knelt before her and took her hands in his. "What are you talking about?" He looked deep into her eyes. "I'm still me. Nothing's changed. This is just another part of my life." He gripped her hands firmly. "Heck, I wasn't that great. The band isn't very good today." A grin curled his lips, and his eyes sparkled.

She laughed and he delivered another megawatt smile. Libby gazed at him, mulling her decision to open up or not. The trust in his eyes made her decision.

"You don't belong with me." It hurt to say it, but she had to tell him the truth.

"What are you talking about?" He sat down, one leg on each side of her, creating a warm cocoon.

"There's a lot you don't know about me."

He nodded in acceptance. "Yeah? There's a lot you don't know about me, too. That's why it's called dating. So we can spend every possible moment together on the phone or pining for each other."

"Stop joking." She sobered, ready to open up for the first time.

"Talk to me, Lib."

"Peter, I'm not the person you think I am." The weight of her confession grew heavier, and she took a deep breath.

"I think I better say this all at once, and I'll tell you when I'm done. Is that okay?"

"Lay it on me," he said with sincerity.

Libby nodded. "I don't live with my mom." She watched him for a reaction and only saw mild confusion. "I live with my aunt. And I'm not from Wisconsin. I'm from Michigan."

She took another deep, bracing breath.

"I have a dad, but I haven't seen him in over a year. He's kind of a mess right now because he lost his job and then our house." She checked Peter again for his reaction; he seemed more confused.

"But he only lost the house because of the accident. Actually, it was way after the accident, after we lost my mom and sister. Did I tell you I had a sister?" She paused and looked into his eyes. He shook his head, his eyes wide and his body still. "Well, she died with my mom in the accident. I guess I never really told you about that." She spoke faster to get the toxic words out. She tugged on her pendant, as Peter listened.

"Well, there was this car accident. My dad was driving, and this semi pulled out, and the driver was tired and, anyway, he forced us off the road and our car flipped over and hit the pillars of an overpass."

She peeked up at his shocked expression.

"There was glass everywhere, and the car was all twisted. It took a while for my dad to help me out of the back where I was stuck. Then he and the truck driver worked on getting my little sister, Sarah, out while I tried to reach my mom."

Libby felt transported back in time to that terrifying summer night on the side of a highway. The night her life changed forever.

"The car was rolled onto the passenger side and was crunched in really bad. My dad was too big to crawl around the twisted metal, so I did."

She remembered the thick metal crumpled like tin foil. It cut and scratched her arms and legs as she fought to get through. She recalled the desperate need to get to her mom, who lay limp, still fastened in her seat, the remnants of the deployed airbag draped around her.

"Chunks of broken glass were everywhere, and I kept trying to pull it away." The taste of panic returned as she recalled the glass spread over her mother like a sheet of deadly crystals. Libby opened her scarred hands to Peter in testament. "But it didn't work."

Peter held her hands in his. It felt good.

"Anyway, it was horrible and I don't live in Michigan anymore, 'cause Dad couldn't take the pain after Mom and Sarah died. He was so depressed, he needed to leave."

Libby couldn't slow herself down.

"That's when he left me at Aunt Marge's, but she's really screwed up and smokes and drinks all day. And I don't know why, but my dad is gone, and I don't know how to find him, so I'm just trying to finish high school so I can figure out what to do. But you need to know this because you have an amazing life and you have a real family with a mom and a dad and brothers."

Peter sat silent, his eyes warm and caring. He took it all in as she babbled.

"So I just thought you should know I'm not like you, and that's okay, and you can go do your thing, and I'm all right with it." She nodded with finality. "I'm all right."

She'd said it all, and now she didn't know what to do. She glanced all around, but avoided beautiful, talented

Peter as long as possible. Finally, she let her eyes meet his.

Pity. She pulled back and crawled away from him. She hated it when others felt pity for her.

"Libby, wait."

She crawled faster. Peter grabbed her leg and rolled her over in the fall leaves. He lay next to her on the ground.

"Libby, stop. It's okay." His eyes were a deep river of concern.

"Don't you dare feel sorry for me. I don't need that. I'm fine." Her jaw set in defiance, but her watering eyes betrayed her.

"Look at me." He held her by the shoulders.

She looked up at him, her rock, her only friend, her whole world.

"It's okay. I don't care about that." He shook his head. "No, I do care about that, but it doesn't matter. It doesn't change anything. You are who you are, and I am who I am. Nothing's changed." He locked eyes with hers and looked deep into her soul. "Your life sucks right now, and mine, well, it doesn't, except that I can't be with you all the time."

He wouldn't let go of her, and she felt so safe. He accepted her past.

"I wish you would have told me before. Why have you held this in?"

"I didn't think you'd want to be with me if you knew how screwed up my life is." Her voice began to quiver.

"Of course I want to know." He pulled her to him and wrapped his famous, talented arms around her.

"It's okay, Lib, I love you, I'm here for you, and I'm not going anywhere."

His words made her feel she might survive after all. She relaxed against him. A rare breath of mourning and pain escaped, and then a single tear. Peter held her tightly, his body enveloping her in a warm embrace of love and understanding.

For the first time in many months, she cried.

• • •

Peter held Libby, crying in his arms. He didn't move, afraid he might frighten her back to her stoic façade. He'd never understood before this moment what loss meant. Here, in his arms, was a girl who'd lost everything. She put on such a strong act, pretending her life was normal, when it was anything but.

But today, she opened up. After all these weeks of pretending, she lowered her guard and let him into her world. He imagined she rarely shared her story, and it explained a lot. No wonder she thought his family so perfect. How could he ever complain about them again when Libby longed for the family she lost?

Peter kissed her salty tears away. Her breath warmed his chest as he held her close. He'd known for a while he was in love with her. She never treated him like a famous rocker. It was always real with her. Libby's confession amped up his determination to protect her and keep her safe. He didn't care about the press or the tabloids or their age. He'd been living the life of an adult for years, and apparently she had, too. Things were about to change.

10

$\mathcal{A}$ quick week later and they were together again, cruising down the highway toward Rockville in a sporty red Jeep. "Nice wheels." Libby ran her fingertips over the butter-soft leather seat.

"Thanks." Peter grinned.

He pushed his hair to the side, unaware of how great he looked. He held the steering wheel casually, the seat belt snug across his narrow hips.

"If you're hoping to keep a low profile, I don't think this is the best way." The flashy red Jeep would stand out in small-town Rockville. The country roads led to the heart of historic downtown.

"I couldn't resist. I can park in a dark alley if you want," Peter said.

"I'm not worried about me; I just figured you wanted to keep things quiet."

"Fans expect to see Jamieson as a group, not one of us out alone wandering middle America. Plus, I brought a hat."

Libby shifted comfortably in her seat. Tonight was just them, flying under the radar. She'd managed to avoid Aunt Marge this afternoon. With any luck, the woman would be strung out and oblivious to Libby's whereabouts. If not, well, Libby didn't care anymore. She'd turn seventeen next summer, and that was practically eighteen.

"Turn right at the stop sign, at Fourth Street. It takes you straight to Main." Her breath caught in her throat at the thought of driving into the heart of town with Peter Jamieson. She felt the need to pinch herself.

They drove down the quiet neighborhood streets lined with giant oaks. Old Victorian homes stood witness as they passed. A bend in the street led them over an old stone bridge and the Rock River.

"This place is amazing. It's like stepping back in time."

"It is pretty." Libby absorbed it with fresh eyes. She always thought of Rockville as a purgatory she'd been forced to endure, not a quaint little town. They drove past the town square, where a pavilion graced the center, and stone benches were scattered in the tree-filled park. Fall leaves coated everything.

"It looks like a cool hangout place. Do you spend much time here?"

"Nope," she answered without regret. "It's too far from

my aunt's house, almost five miles. I ride the bus to school and don't have my license, let alone a car to drive." She stopped asking permission to get her license months ago. Aunt Marge said it would only lead to bad behavior. At first, Libby didn't care about getting her license. She worried driving might be a constant reminder of the accident. The pungent smell of gasoline at the crash still haunted her. However, her tolerance of Aunt Marge's bizarre rules was wearing thin. Since the issue with her dad's letters, she couldn't care less what her aunt said or thought.

"That's why I hang out at Parfrey's Glen. Anywhere else is too far."

Peter reached over and held her hand, which amazed her every time. It was as if he could transfer all his strength and confidence to her.

After a turn onto Main Street and past a handful of shops, the lights of Ed's Drive-in appeared.

"That must be it." Peter approached the drive-up restaurant. A handful of cars occupied spots, each with food trays attached to their windows.

"Yep." Libby nodded.

"This is going to be fun." Peter pulled into the lot and parked farthest from the restaurant and the bulk of the other cars.

After checking out the menu, Peter placed their order through a little metal box with a crackly speaker.

"Get cheese curds, too," Libby added.

Peter gave her a crooked look. "It's a Wisconsin thing, right?"

"Oh yeah." She and her dad shared some here the day he dropped her off.

They sat in the Jeep and talked about everything and nothing at all, oblivious to the other diners. When the food arrived, the twenty-something waitress looked twice at Peter but said nothing. As she walked away, she glanced back at him and then Libby, obviously weighing the likelihood of the recognized face belonging to the real Peter Jamieson.

"People don't expect to see me, so they don't."

Peter was here to see Libby and she wanted everyone in town to know it, but she didn't want to share him, either. She coveted their every moment.

Together, they stuffed themselves with greasy food until Libby thought she'd burst. She couldn't remember the last time she'd eaten out.

"So you aren't one of those girls who barely eats on a date?"

"Why wouldn't I eat?" She sucked the last of her chocolate malt from the bottom of the glass, creating a hollow suction sound with her straw.

Peter laughed. "I don't know. I guess some girls don't want guys to see them eating."

Libby stirred the straw around the glass, scooting the last bits of malt together. "I love food." She handed the empty glass back for him to place on the tray.

"Where to next?" Peter asked.

"First, the waitress needs to come get the tray off the side of the door. Otherwise, I guarantee you will be noticed driving down the street with a food tray hanging on your window."

"Oh yeah, guess I missed that little detail."

His brief look of embarrassment warmed her heart. The world traveler, Peter Jamieson, didn't know how to do a drive-up restaurant. "Start the car or turn your lights on. She'll come."

Peter started the Jeep; the powerful engine hummed. Within a couple minutes, the waitress returned for their tray. As she lifted it from the window, she eyed Peter again.

"You wouldn't happen to be—"

"Nope," Peter interrupted, then flashed her his famous smile as he put the Jeep in reverse.

The waitress stepped out of the way. Libby saw her glance down at the tray and see the twenty-dollar tip. She looked up at him, her face more confused than ever. Peter backed up and then pulled onto Main Street.

"Which direction is the Trivoli?"

"We're going to a movie?" Libby hadn't seen a movie in ages.

"Of course. It wouldn't be a proper date if we didn't have dinner and a movie."

Libby couldn't have asked for a more perfect night. She

directed him farther down Main. They had a half hour before the show started, so Peter parked and they wandered along the river.

"So how did you convince your parents to let you come?" She looped her arm around his.

"I held them at gunpoint," he said with a straight face.

"No, really?" She poked him in the arm.

"It wasn't hard at all . . . considering it's my eighteenth birthday."

Libby stopped. "It's your birthday? When?" She faced him and blocked his path.

"Today."

"You didn't tell me!" She grabbed the front of his leather jacket and tried to give him a good shake.

"What was I supposed to say?" he said, laughing. "It's my birthday, so you have to be really nice to me and bake me a cake?"

"Yes, that's exactly what you were supposed to say," she brooded. "I would have gotten you a present." How, she didn't know. It would have been worth the punishment of cleaning the school lunchroom again.

"Spending time with you is all the present I need." He put his arm around her and pulled her close.

"Well, you need a birthday present. Eighteen is a big deal. When I turn eighteen, the world is going to know."

"My life is filled with 'over the top.' I wanted something meaningful."

Libby gazed into his gorgeous eyes, then reached and brought his face down to hers. She kissed him sweetly on the mouth. It felt like her birthday today, not his. She reached behind her neck and unhooked her necklace.

"I know this isn't much, but it's one of my favorite things. If it isn't too dorky or weird, I'd like you to have it." She held the pendant out for him. It was one of her most prized possessions.

He touched the onyx carving, strung on a leather cord, and his eyes connected with hers. "Are you sure?"

"Yes," she stated. "It's some ancient symbol. It means 'believe.'"

"It's awesome. Very rock and roll." He rubbed his thumb over the smooth stone.

"You think?" Libby nibbled at her lip. She wanted him to love it as much as she did.

"Yeah." He touched the tip of her nose with his. "Where'd you get it?"

"My mom gave it to me after a trip she and my dad took." She liked how the leather cord lay against Peter's skin.

Peter sighed, his tone serious. "Oh, Libby, are you sure?" His eyes searched hers. "It's too important."

"If you don't want it, that's okay, but if you do, I'd love for you to have it. I don't think it's very girly—I think it was actually meant for a guy—but Mom and I thought it was cool."

"Yes, I want it." He closed his hand over hers. "And it isn't girly at all. I wondered why you always wore it."

Libby squeezed his hand, glad to share this connection. Her mom would have liked him a lot.

"Help me." Peter leaned close.

She placed the thin leather cord around his neck and attached the clasp, then stood back. Satisfied, she nodded. "I like it." Her neck felt bare without it, but on Peter the pendant looked perfect, as if created for him alone.

Peter touched the carving against his skin. "Me too." He leaned down and kissed her, sending little thrills through her body.

They left the river behind and meandered down Main Street, his arm slung over her shoulder, and her head resting against him.

"The town is so quiet. Where is everybody on a Friday night?"

"At the football game. The town practically shuts down for Friday night football."

"Would you rather go to the game?"

"No way. Those people mean nothing to me. Plus, you don't have to worry about getting recognized. Everyone under the age of forty is at the game."

"Why don't they mean anything to you?"

"I wasn't born and raised here, and my aunt is a total wack job, so that doesn't help. They know about my family." She stopped talking for a minute. Peter looked down at her, his face sincere. "They don't know the details, just that Mom died and Dad left me here."

Talking about her family hurt. She missed them so much. Her throat tightened.

"Hey, you're not alone anymore. Okay?" He stopped, his eyes focused on hers.

"Okay." They began walking again. Peter put his arm around her and held her close.

She slid her arm around his waist and hooked her thumb in the edge of his back pocket. It felt nice to belong again.

• • •

After the movie, Peter drove them back toward the stifling farmhouse. His gut ached thinking of leaving Libby with her aunt who apparently drank all day.

"Are you sure you're okay there?"

"It's fine. I'm used to it." She sighed.

"Well, I've been thinking. . . . Actually, there are two things. First, I think we need to get you out of here." There, he'd said it.

"What are you talking about?" She sat upright and stared at him through the dark.

"It's terrible for you here. You have no ties to anything except your psycho aunt. She sounds like bad news, and honestly, I'm surprised your dad would leave you with her."

Libby sat silent and contemplated his words. He knew they struck close to home.

"I'm sorry, that was cruel. I'm sure your dad did what he thought best." Peter couldn't imagine how a father could leave his own daughter. If he ever lost Libby, he'd go insane.

"It's okay. I know what you mean. He wasn't in his right mind. I tried to get him to take me with him, but he wouldn't. He seemed to just shut down. He rarely ate and lost a lot of weight. Something inside him just broke."

"Grief is a powerful thing, and you both lost a lot. Listen, I'm eighteen now, and I want you to come be with me. You'd be safer."

Peter could picture how much fun they'd have together and how happy Libby would be away from Rockville. He hoped she agreed.

She sat, wide-eyed. She opened her mouth to speak and then stopped. He could almost see the wheels turning in her mind.

"I would love to escape this town and be together 24/7, but how would we do that? Where would I live? Would I go on tour with you?" Libby asked the same questions that rolled around his mind.

"I haven't got it figured out, but I'm working on it, and it's going to take some time before I can make it happen."

"Peter, I'd love to run away with you, but somehow I don't think your family would be too keen about some strange girl showing up. What about school? And what about my dad? He's coming back for me. I know he is."

Peter wanted to say that if he hadn't come back in the past year, it wasn't likely he'd return any time soon, but he kept it to himself.

"I know. It's a lot to think about. You're in a bad situation, surrounded by people who don't care about you, but I care, and I want you with me." He reached for her hand and held it firmly. "I've got all kinds of money, and it should be good for something. Maybe it can help get you outta here."

"That's the nicest thing anyone has ever said to me. I'm so happy, I could cry."

"Good. I don't think I could take any more tears. When you live in a house with four guys, crying doesn't exist. Garrett beat that out of me when I was three."

"So what was the other thing you wanted to tell me about?"

Peter couldn't wait to lay this one on her. "I think we should go to your homecoming dance." He watched for her reaction.

Libby stared at him, her mouth agape. "You're nuts. You just agreed I have nothing here, and now you want to go to the Rockville homecoming?"

"Why not go? You mentioned homecoming earlier and I never got the chance to go to a school dance. Don't you think it's something everyone should do once? It would be normal. I never get to be normal, and think how surprised everyone will be to see you with me."

"Aren't we a little full of ourselves?" she teased. "Actually they would be shocked to see me with a date at all. Heck, they'd be shocked to see me out after five o'clock."

"Then it's a date." He wanted Libby by his side. He wanted to show the world his beautiful girlfriend.

"I think you're crazy. How do you know you can even make it? What if you have a concert or something?"

"If I have a concert, then obviously it won't work. I guess we'll have to crash some other school's dance. Get the date, and we'll figure it out from there."

"I'll have to deal with the crazy aunt issue. I'm not sure how tonight is going to go over. I might be locked in the castle tower for the next month."

"Then I'll come rescue you." And he would. Anywhere. Anytime.

"Deal."

Peter drove past the entry to the preserve.

"Where are you going? You need to drop me off."

"I'm not dropping you off in the woods late at night. I assume your aunt's place is up ahead."

"Yeah, but don't go there. Drop me off at the corner. I don't want her to see you."

"No." He turned onto the side road that led to the old farmhouse and slowly pulled into the driveway, and then faced Libby.

"This was the best night of my life, you know," she said.

"Me too." Their date far outshone any concert he had ever played. They leaned close, and he put his hand behind her neck, held her gently, and kissed her good night.

Suddenly, Libby's door whipped open, and light flooded the Jeep. A crazed woman, who must be her aunt, glared at them. The whites of her eyes stood out next to her yellowing teeth. Libby cringed and leaned away.

"Where've you been?" the woman shrieked.

11

Libby looked from her aunt to Peter and back. "Out with a friend."

"You thought I wouldn't notice you snuck out, did you? You lied to me. I knew you would. First time I let down my guard, and you're off screwing some boy."

Shock didn't begin to describe how Peter felt. This woman was an unbalanced lunatic.

Libby looked to Peter, horror on her face. "I gotta go."

"Are you sure?" He grabbed her hand and held on tight, afraid to let her go.

She nodded. Her eyes filled with conflict as she pulled away.

"I'll call you," he whispered as Libby hurried out of the Jeep.

"What did he say?" her aunt badgered.

Libby closed the door, looked back at him, and mouthed, "I'm sorry."

Her aunt stalked behind her, yelling colorful phrases as Peter watched. He could tell Libby wanted the scene over with.

Aunt Marge paused her screaming long enough to glance back and see he hadn't left the driveway. She spun toward him.

"What are you waiting for? Get the hell off my property!"

Peter threw the Jeep in reverse, pulled out, and returned the way he came. It took all the strength he had not to turn around and go get her. *Damn it.* He slammed his hand on the steering wheel. How could he leave Libby here? He needed to find a way to get her out and soon.

Once out of sight, he turned the headlights off and parked the car so he could watch the house from a distance. A few minutes later, he saw an upstairs light go on. He continued to watch the house, to make sure Libby's aunt didn't notice the Jeep and come back with a shotgun.

He pressed redial on his phone. A moment later, Libby's sweet voice filled his ears. "Oh God, Peter, I'm so sorry."

"Are you okay?"

"I'm okay, don't worry," Libby whispered.

But he did worry. "Are you sure it's safe? Do you want me to come back and get you? I hate that you have to stay with her."

"I don't think that would be the best way to go. Let's plan it out, otherwise we might have the police on our tail."

"Libby, she's scary." He wanted to say she was a psycho freak who shouldn't be allowed out in public, let alone near kids, but he didn't want to upset Libby more. She wasn't given a choice when her dad dumped her with the woman.

"I know. Usually, she's ultra-mellow and semi passed out. She must have been drinking all night. That's when she gets mean."

"God, Libby, you can't stay there. I don't trust her." He pushed a hand through his hair in frustration.

"It'll be okay. Where are you?"

"I'm pulled over about a hundred yards down the road. I can see the light of your bedroom window."

"I'd ask you to flash your lights, but Lady Paranoia might blow a gasket."

"Can you stay on the phone for a while?" It was the next best thing to being with her.

"All night if you want, but you better get started back. Birthday or not, you don't need to get in trouble, too."

• • •

A couple of days later, Libby wanted to crawl under the dash of Miss Orman's car. Her counselor insisted she give Libby a ride home to talk to Aunt Marge about the homecoming dance. It was just the other day Aunt Marge had blown up over the Peter incident. The last thing Libby needed was more drama with her aunt. The tires crunched on the gravel as Miss Orman pulled in.

"Don't worry, it's going to be fine." Miss Orman shot her a reassuring look. Libby hoped she was right.

Miss Orman stepped out of her car and walked to the front of the farmhouse as Aunt Marge appeared from the barn, wiping her hands on her faded plaid shirt. She didn't look happy as she pulled the heavy door closed and secured it with a padlock. Libby didn't know if she should stay with Miss Orman or wait for Aunt Marge. She really just wanted to go hide in her room to avoid the inevitable scene.

Aunt Marge trudged through tall grass to the front of the house. Wet grass from a recent rain licked at her beat-up boots.

"What do you want?" Marge barked.

Miss Orman jumped, almost losing her purse in the process. "Oh, I didn't see you there." Collecting herself, she offered a slender hand. "Hi, I'm Julie Orman, we met last year when—"

"I know who you are. What do you want?" Rumpled Aunt Marge glared at the woman in the creased slacks and stylish heels.

"I wanted to speak to you about Libby."

"What'd she do now? I doubt she'd dare steal again, but if you like, I can punish her some more." Aunt Marge sneered at Libby, who wished she were invisible.

Miss Orman looked horrified. "No, nothing like that, and Libby has already completed her in-school punishment. Actually, what I'm here about is more of an opportunity."

Aunt Marge immediately lost interest. "I was working. Call me later." Her aunt turned to head back to the barn.

Miss Orman followed on Aunt Marge's heavy heels. "I've been calling for the past few days, and you never answer my calls or return my messages."

"Like I said, I have a lot of work to do and don't have time to chitty-chat about the girl."

"This won't take more than a few minutes. It's very important to Libby." Miss Orman cast Libby a hopeful look.

As they walked around the edge of the house, Miss Orman carefully stepped through the damp grass as they approached the barn. Aunt Marge stopped in her tracks.

"Do you work in there?" Miss Orman asked, indicating the dilapidated barn. "What do you do?"

Aunt Marge clenched her teeth.

Good question. Libby had never paid attention to what Aunt Marge did before. She just knew she disappeared a lot. She was always relieved when her aunt wasn't around and never thought more of it.

"I make soap," Aunt Marge barked, and glared at Miss Orman.

The surprise etched on Miss Orman's face matched Libby's.

"How wonderful! Libby never mentioned your business. Where do you sell it? I'd love to buy some."

Aunt Marge grunted in reply, then turned back toward the front of the house. They followed her like children wanting a favor from their parents. Aunt Marge pulled keys from her saggy denim pocket and unlocked the door. One good shove and it opened. She entered, then turned abruptly. "Get on with it. What do you want?"

"Oh," Miss Orman responded, gripping her purse. "Libby doesn't get a lot of interaction with other students."

"She's at school all day. What the hell do you call that?"

"Actually, Libby keeps to herself a lot, and she is carrying a very heavy course load with all her honors and AP classes."

Aunt Marge watched Miss Orman peer around the entryway and into the cluttered living room and kitchen. Libby could see her aunt's temper rising.

Even though Libby had cleaned up a few days ago, Aunt Marge's trash already littered the tables and counters. Her counselor's gaze took in everything.

"Get to the point." Aunt Marge pulled Miss Orman's attention back to her.

Miss Orman stood straighter and assumed an authoritative air. "Homecoming is next week, and Libby needs to attend."

"You came all the way out here and interrupted my work so that kid can go to a dance?"

"Yes, it's part of her high school experience. Every student should enjoy this rite of passage."

"I never went to a school dance, and it didn't hurt me a bit."

Libby doubted anyone ever invited her.

"Hey, I took the kid in. I think that's more than enough," Aunt Marge said.

"But Libby has been through a traumatic time. She's lost her family. She needs as many normal teenage experiences as possible. She doesn't have a job. She doesn't have a driver's license. All these things are important to a young person's development."

Libby slunk away toward the stairs and hopefully out of Aunt Marge's sight. Her aunt did not like to be told what to do.

"Driving costs money, and she's already a financial drain. Now you want me to give her money to buy a fancy dress?" Aunt Marge crossed her arms, clearly ready to shut Miss Orman down.

Instead of being intimidated, Miss Orman stepped into the kitchen, where a couple flies flitted around old fast-food containers. She opened the bare refrigerator, revealing dried-up food on plates alongside a few bottles of forgotten condiments.

"Don't worry about a dress. I'll take care of it." She shut the fridge door.

"You can't come in here and tell me what to do. I'm

her legal guardian. I know how kids her age act. Once you let them loose, there's no stopping them. She'll end up knocked up, just like her mother."

Libby's jaw dropped. She wanted to scream "liar!" Her parents had been married a year and a half before Libby was born.

"I'll be chaperoning the dance, so she'll be with me the entire time. I'll pick her up that afternoon and return her home after the dance. You don't need to do a thing."

The two women stood their ground, Aunt Marge in her dirty work clothes and Miss Orman in her designer blouse and slacks. Both refused to look away.

"When was the last time the social worker completed a home visit?" Miss Orman's eyes lit in challenge.

Libby had never seen Miss Orman so tough. She liked having someone on her side like this. She wanted to cheer as Aunt Marge's blood practically boiled.

"You damn school people think you can intrude whenever you want, and all in the name of child welfare." She wavered. "Fine, take her, but I'm not giving her a dime."

A smirk appeared on Miss Orman's unblemished face. She moved to open the front door. "Thank you. Libby will be in good hands." She stepped outside.

Aunt Marge followed. "One more thing. Don't ever step on my property again." She slammed the aging door in Miss Orman's face.

Libby shrank against the stair railing.

"You think you're so smart, sending in the big guns so you can go to your little dance. Well, you better watch your step, missy. You're getting mighty close to the flame." Aunt Marge pierced Libby with a venomous stare. "Get out of my sight."

12

"*Hair* up or down?"

A week later on the night of the homecoming dance, Libby perched on a kitchen stool in the small bathroom of Miss Orman's apartment. Hair and makeup paraphernalia cluttered the tiny counter.

"Both," she answered. "I want the front and sides up and then the back to fall in a bunch of curls. Can we do that?"

"We can do anything." Miss Orman studied Libby's long hair, determining how best to begin.

Sitting together in front of the giant mirror reminded Libby of the times she watched her mother get ready for special parties with her dad. She and Sarah would sit on the counter and laundry hamper playing with her mom's cosmetics. They laughed and teased each other as Mom artfully applied makeup, occasionally brushing blush on their faces or spritzing them with perfume. Libby smiled to herself at the memory.

Miss Orman brushed through Libby's hair; her summer highlights still shimmered. Libby closed her eyes and imagined it was Mom who held the brush and hummed as she worked. Perhaps she peered down from the heavens to guide Libby through this memorable day.

"Have you decided which dress?"

Miss Orman had borrowed two dresses from a friend's daughter. Libby didn't care if she wore a used dress; she was ecstatic to be going. Plus, the dresses were beautiful.

"I like the pink-and-brown one." It fit close to her body and then flowed loosely over her hips and legs. The top tied behind her neck like a halter top and revealed her back. The front showed just the right amount of cleavage. She felt as if she had transformed into a beautiful girl when she tried it on.

"That's my favorite, too. I like how the patterns swirl together. Plus, you look amazing in it. Any boy would be crazy not to fall at your feet," Miss Orman said, using the curling iron on Libby's long locks.

"You think so?" Libby blushed, but for once it was out of excitement instead of humiliation.

She wondered what it would be like to spend an entire evening with Peter, dancing in his arms and letting the world see they belonged together. After losing her family, she gave up on her dreams, but now, with Peter in her life, everything had changed. He made dreaming possible again.

"The boys at school won't know who you are. Everyone is so used to shy, quiet you. I can just imagine how surprised they will be to see you. You are going to have a great time." Miss Orman tugged on a lock of Libby's hair and smiled.

They continued their preparations and chatted away the time. Libby and Peter wouldn't be going out to dinner. He couldn't get there until shortly after the dance started, but she didn't care. It was a miracle he could attend at all. Miss Orman offered to drive, since she was a chaperone for the night. Even Aunt Marge cooperated in allowing the night to happen. Everything fell perfectly into place.

After they split a pizza, and Libby put the final touches on her makeup, Miss Orman zipped her into the beautiful dress. Libby barely recognized herself in the full-length mirror. A gorgeous young woman stood poised and confident before her. Libby turned to Miss Orman in disbelief.

"You look stunning," Miss Orman said.

Libby flung herself into the woman's arms. "Thank you."

"It's all you." Miss Orman hugged her warmly. "And it's

been there all the time. Now, when do I finally get to meet this mystery man?"

Just then Libby's phone rang. They looked at each other and laughed.

. . .

"I'm here! We just landed." Peter carried a small duffel bag over his shoulder and a bag with Libby's corsage of pink roses and daisies in his hand.

Roger walked ahead of him up the gangway as they exited the plane.

"Oh my God, I can't believe this is really happening." Libby's voice bubbled from his phone.

"I know, me neither. I told you we'd figure this out." His excitement rivaled hers.

"So how much longer?"

"About an hour if we drive the speed limit, forty-five minutes if I have anything to say about it." He wanted Libby in his arms. This long-distance thing was killing him, but she was worth it.

"Guess I better get going or you'll beat me there. I can't wait to see the look on everyone's face when you walk in. Good thing you have Roger with you."

"Roger loves his job so much right now. He can't wait to get there and try out his dance moves with the high school set. Wait till you see what he's wearing."

Roger turned and growled at Peter. The only dress jacket they could find at the last minute to fit his large frame was dark purple velvet. He looked like a flashback from the disco era.

Libby giggled. "Well, hurry up."

Roger stopped him as they entered the gate area. A serious-looking airport official and security guard approached.

"Hey, I gotta go, something's up, probably some security thing. I'll see you in an hour."

"Hurry."

He flipped the phone shut and stepped forward to speak to the official.

• • •

The loud bass from the cover band pumped into the corridor.

"Are you sure you don't want to come in and enjoy the dance?" Miss Orman urged again, their earlier excitement long faded.

"No. I'll wait here." Libby refused to go into the gym with the other kids. When Peter arrived, she needed to be the first to lay eyes on him. No way would she miss the moment by standing alone in the darkened, Hollywood-themed gym.

"He must have had car trouble," her counselor offered.

Concern, even pity etched Miss Orman's face.

"Yeah, probably. Maybe a flat tire." Libby nodded, her lips pinched with worry.

Something had obviously happened. Everything seemed fine when they talked two hours earlier. If a swarm of fans was the holdup, she swore she'd kill them all. Peter belonged to her tonight and no one else.

She paced the long hallway again, the click of her ill-fitted heels echoed with each step. She lowered herself onto a bench and checked her phone yet again for messages.

No power. Crap.

She'd been distracted all day and forgot to recharge it. Her only connection to Peter lay useless in her hand. Unfortunately, her phone charger was hidden behind books on a shelf in her room. She couldn't charge her phone without going back to the house, and then Aunt Marge would never let her out again. It was a big enough battle to leave the first time.

Two girls in slinky, sequined dresses walked out of the bathroom and meandered down the hall. They eyed Libby.

"Why's she sitting there alone?" the tall girl who wore super high heels asked.

"I think her date stood her up," replied the other with bright lipstick.

"I would totally die if that happened to me," said the girl, wobbling on her heels.

Libby slouched against the wall. Her once-beautiful curls drooped against her shoulders. Their words hit hard, but they were right. He wasn't coming. She knew it in her gut. Their perfect night, ruined. Peter would not show. Tonight, she had planned to prove she was just like everyone else, even better. Instead, they would all witness her lonely wait for a boy who never arrived. Miss Orman's pity would be the worst. She'd probably call in a shrink on Monday to find out why Libby had invented Peter.

As more kids walked down the hall toward the restrooms, Libby exited through the double doors and stepped into the brisk night. Even though she felt certain Peter wouldn't show, she continued her vigil and prayed he was okay.

What could possibly keep him away when he was so close? *A traffic jam? Not likely. Weather?* He'd already landed, and the weather was fine, cold and windy, but nothing to stop traffic. *A car accident?* She shivered at the thought. *Please let him be okay.*

She checked her phone again. It didn't magically power on. She returned it to her handbag, next to her lip gloss and two tickets for the dance. She pulled out the beautifully printed tickets with the school emblem pressed into the shiny paper.

"Oh, Peter," she breathed, the wind cold on her skin. Something was very, very wrong.

13

"*Excuse* me, are you Peter Jamieson?" asked an airline employee.

"Yeah, I'm Peter Jamieson," he answered slowly, a bad feeling creeping over him. "What's up?"

"I'm sorry to tell you this, but there's been a medical emergency back in Los Angeles. Your mother called and asked us to locate you. You need to return to LA as quickly as possible."

"What happened? Who is it?" Panic hit him full on. He searched Roger's face for information neither of them had.

"Is it my mom? Is she okay?" Peter stood, oblivious to the dozens of curious passengers in the terminal. The only reason his mom would make him come home was if something terrible happened.

"I'm sorry to tell you that your father suffered a heart attack. I believe he's in the emergency room at Cedars-Sinai."

Peter's world fell away. His dad. The man who pushed him to be his best. He couldn't be sick; he was the rock of their family. Peter looked to Roger for support, terrified for his father's life.

"How soon can we get out of here?" Roger said, taking control.

"We're holding a plane that's headed to Denver. Then you'll transfer to LA. You can board now."

"Let's go," Peter responded. "I'm calling Garrett."

Stiff-jawed, he pressed the buttons on his phone as he followed the officials through the terminal to the waiting plane.

Garrett answered on the first ring. "Where the hell are you?"

"I'm on my way now. We just landed in Madison, but they're holding a plane. How is he? What happened?" Peter didn't recognize the flat tone of his own voice. He fought tears as he rushed down the concourse. His invincible dad had always been healthy. This was all wrong.

"He was walking across the yard and collapsed. Mom gave him an aspirin right away. The paramedics said it probably saved his life."

Peter held the phone with one hand and pushed his

hair out of his face with the other. He struggled to grasp what Garrett was telling him. "Is he okay? Where is he now?" They arrived at a gate where airline agents waited. One agent handed him a boarding pass and cleared him through without delay. Peter nodded his gratitude as he listened to Garrett.

"They're doing a lot of tests. He's hooked up to a bunch of machines. Mom's with him."

"Is he going to be okay?" Peter couldn't believe he needed to ask this.

"I don't know, Pete," Garrett said softly. The worry in his voice scared Peter even more.

"Is Adam with you?" Peter stepped onto the crowded plane. Impatient passengers watched. He and Roger were guided to seats near the front.

"Yeah, he's right here. How long until you land? Damn it, Peter. You should be here."

"I know. I'm on my way. A couple hours to Denver and a couple more to LA. Hopefully by midnight." He checked his watch and dreaded the idea of being stuck on a plane for the rest of the night helpless to do anything. He needed to be there. Now.

"Just get your ass home. You never should have left. She isn't worth it."

Peter ignored the barb. Garrett was scared and angry. So was he. "I'll be there soon. I'll call when we land in

Denver." The door closed, and the plane taxied the short distance to the runway. "Garrett, don't let him die." He spoke softly, not wanting to hang up. There was no reply for the longest time as the two brothers shared a frightened silence.

"Just hurry." The tone of Garrett's voice told Peter all he needed to know.

Peter ended the call and sniffed back his emotions. His throat tightened and he closed his eyes to fight back his tears. Roger squeezed his arm in support. In private, Peter might have hugged the big man and cried. Instead, he put on a brave face as the flight attendants finished the safety talk and did their final check for takeoff.

Suddenly, he opened his eyes. "Libby!"

Damn it, he'd forgotten all about her. He opened the phone again, about to press DIAL, when the flight attendant stopped him.

"I'm sorry. You need to turn that off. We're about to take off and it interferes with in-flight communications."

"But it'll only take a second. It's important." He had to make a call to Libby. He couldn't leave her standing at the dance alone, wondering where he was. They'd worked so hard to make this happen. She'd suffered so much in the past year, and he wanted to bring her happiness. Instead, she'd be devastated.

"I'm sorry, but it's airline policy. No exceptions."

"Put it away, Peter. She'll understand," Roger said calmly.

Peter didn't like it, but he turned the phone off and slid it into his pocket. He slammed his head against the cushioned first-class seat in frustration.

14

Libby stared blankly out her bedroom window toward Parfrey's Glen and listened again to her messages that Peter had left during a layover on his way back to LA. His voice sounded strained and worried. He was so sorry. It tore at her heart. The emotion in his voice brought back the old memories and pain. During the hours after her family's car crash, she had felt the same way, as piercing dread overwhelmed her. She'd experienced numbness and the taste of fear.

She crawled onto her bed, not bothering to take off the homecoming dress. She curled on her side and clasped the phone against her heart. She cried for Peter, his family, and all the fear she understood too clearly. She cried for his father's suffering as he fought for his life. And she cried for herself.

She let the floodgates open and mourned the loss of her

mom and her sister. She cried because she would never get ready for a party with them. Her mom would never meet Peter and never see her graduate high school. She cried because of what her life had once been and would never be again.

She released tears of frustration at being dumped at her aunt's lonely, loveless house. She missed her dad so much, but felt angry that he abandoned her. She cried for her lack of friends and freedom. She'd put on a brave front for so long, but now the façade crumbled. Finally, she cried for herself and Peter, both robbed of a normal childhood, for very different reasons. Tonight was to be their time, their turn, just a simple evening together.

Never in her life had she felt so alone.

• • •

The days following the botched homecoming dance and his dad's heart attack flew by. The heart specialists assured the family that his dad was out of danger but needed to rest. In an attempt to force his dad to take it easy, Peter's mom rented a house on Venice Beach in California. Life fell back into a normal pattern of concerts, interviews, and regular calls to Libby. Peter still felt awful about standing her up at homecoming, but she told him to stop apologizing; family should always come first.

If there was an upside to the heart attack, it was Peter's sudden freedom from his parents. His mom spent all her time hovering while his dad became more ornery over his new diet and restricted activity.

Peter pulled on a baseball hat, grabbed the earpiece for his phone, and slid on a pair of sunglasses. "Going for a run," he yelled as he left. After a few warm-up stretches, he stepped through the dry sand and punched in Libby's number. When he hit the packed sand near the low morning tide, he broke into a jog. The salty scent of ocean air filled his senses. He loved spending time on the coast.

"You're right on time," Libby answered.

Peter smiled. The sound of her voice always made his day, like when a great song popped into his head. "Yeah, well, I'm still sucking up so you won't dump me."

"Stop it. I've told you a million times, it's okay. How's your dad today?"

"Better than ever. My mother's been driving him nuts with all her attention. Every time he starts to work, she threatens to call 911. He sees the doctor for a follow-up tomorrow. I think Mom is loving every minute of control until the doctor gives him the okay to work again."

"That's great he's doing so well."

"Yeah, but he's always blasting the TV. To annoy my mom, he's been watching Charlie's Angels movies over and over. It's driving her nuts." Peter loved his dad's tactics.

"My mom loved the *Charlie's Angels* television show. She used to watch it when she was a little girl. In fact, she

wanted to name me Jill after Jill Munroe, one of the char-
acters, but my dad wouldn't let her."

"You, a Jill? I don't think so. Libby is much spunkier.
Fits you better."

"Plus, I don't have the sex appeal of the actress that
played her."

"Now there I'll disagree." Libby was more beautiful
than any movie star. She just didn't know it, which he loved
about her.

"You're sucking up again."

"Never!" He laughed.

"Okay, and now you're breathing heavy. Where are you
running today?"

He dodged a woman walking a fluffy little dog. "The
beach. Where are you?"

"Just arriving at Parfrey's Glen."

"I wish I was there."

"Well, I wish I was in Southern California on a warm
beach, not blustery late November in Wisconsin. All the
leaves are off the trees and everything looks dead and cold.
It could snow any minute."

He imagined her bundled up against the cold, holding
the collar of her coat closed so the sharp wind wouldn't
bite so hard. He pictured her rosy cheeks and windblown
hair. "I know, but hang tough. It won't be long now, and
you won't have to live there anymore. Did you fill out the

passport forms yet?" He'd been hatching a plan to get her out. If things went his way, she'd join him on their European tour and finish high school via homeschooling like he did.

"They're filled out, but I don't know how we'll get them signed without a parent."

"Don't worry. I'm working on it. Once my mom isn't so freaked out about my dad, I'll tell her everything. There is no way she won't step forward and help. When she sees an injustice, she'll move heaven and earth to fix it. She'll deal with your aunt and take over guardianship."

"Are you sure? She's never even met me. Why would she do that?"

"Because she cares about me, and she always supports everything I do. You're part of my life and living with your aunt can't continue." His mom had the biggest heart, and he knew she'd be moved by Libby's situation. He hadn't mentioned it before because he wanted to respect Libby's privacy. But the more he learned about her home life, the more he worried.

"I can't believe you're going to get me out of here. It's like a fairy tale and you're going to rescue me from the evil queen."

"Yeah, I'll have to get my white horse out of the stable to make it complete." He dodged a rogue wave that washed ashore and threatened to soak him.

"You are so full of yourself," she teased.

He grinned at the sarcasm in her voice. "So, what are you up to today?" The beach became more crowded by the minute. He'd have to return soon.

"When I get back, there's a research paper waiting. That should fill the rest of the day," Libby said.

"What a drag. How about Cruella De Vil? Has she been hassling you?"

"Nah, she's been out in the barn all weekend. I don't know what she's doing out there. She says she's making soap, but I've never seen any, and trust me, she could use more soap."

"Well, anything that keeps her away from you makes me happy."

"What are you doing today, besides hanging out at the beach in the warm sun and making me jealous?"

Three little boys dashed in front of him toward the water. Peter dodged them. "Garrett's got phone interviews set for most of the day. With Dad on the mend, Garrett's decided he needs to be king of the mountain and run my life. I'm just about ready to take him out. He's been riding me every minute. Suddenly, he thinks that if we miss even one opportunity for an interview or appearance, our careers will end up in the toilet."

"Sounds like he's just looking out for the band," Libby said.

"No, Garrett only looks out for himself. I think it's all about having control. He's power hungry and loves to run my life."

"He can't be that bad."

"You have no idea. He can be a real asshole when he wants."

Peter talked to Libby until time ran out and he needed to rush back and shower. A day of marathon phone interviews lay ahead. The only good part was that he and his brothers didn't have to go anywhere. The interviews would be done from the beach house.

Garrett waited for him on the deck when he returned.

"You're late," Garrett growled. "You can't tell me you were out running all that time. You sitting in a coffee shop talking to Libby again?"

"None of your business. I don't have to tell you anything. And ya know what? You need to relax. You should go work out and try to get that stick out of your ass. It might help improve your glowing personality."

"And you need to dump your dead weight in Wisconsin," Garrett said as Peter pushed past.

• • •

Libby was surprised a week later when her phone rang while she was waiting for the bus. When she saw Peter's name pop up on the screen, she smiled and answered.

"Hey! I didn't expect to hear from you until tonight."

She walked around the side of the house so Aunt Marge wouldn't see her with the phone.

"This isn't Peter," responded a flat voice.

"Who is this?"

"It's Garrett. Peter's brother," he snapped.

"Oh. What's up? Where's Peter?" She didn't like the tone in Garrett's voice. Something was wrong.

"Well, that's just it. He asked me to call you."

Libby's heart dropped. "Is he okay?"

"He's fine. I mean, nothing happened to him or anything."

"So, what's going on?" She walked behind the farmhouse where she could talk louder.

"Listen, I'm gonna say this straight out." He cleared his throat. "Peter didn't know how to tell you this, and he didn't want you to go all psycho or anything, so he asked me to do it."

Her stomach hurt. Peter could tell her anything. They were so close and talked about everything. Libby's mind flashed from one tragic thought to the next.

"The tour is really crazy, and it's too hard to keep things going with you when he needs to be working. So, anyway, he won't be calling anymore, and it would be best if you don't call him, either."

Suddenly, her world moved in slow motion. This could not be happening. "What are you saying? Is Peter breaking up with me?" Libby's chest tightened. This made no sense.

Garrett was wrong. Peter loved her. In a few more days, he was coming to get her. They had a plan. He was eighteen now, and she would travel with him.

Garrett cleared his throat again. "Yeah. That's pretty much it."

Libby couldn't believe what she was hearing. She couldn't imagine Peter asking Garrett to be the one to break her heart. She needed to hear it from Peter. "Let me talk to him. Give Peter the phone."

"He's not here. He left already. Look, Peter and I don't always get along, but we're devoted to the band. This is business; it's not personal."

She found it difficult to breathe.

"Peter would never do this. He's coming to get me in three days. We have a plan. You're lying!"

"Whatever plans you think he made with you aren't going to happen. It's over, Libby. He had fun, you had fun, but don't you read the tabloids? This happens all the time. He has more important things to do than hang out with some girl from Hicksville."

"That's not true. He loves me," she cried.

"Whoa. Back it up. What fantasy world are you living in? What makes you think someone like Peter would be in love with you? He has everything. He doesn't need you, and he's done hanging out in your small-town world. It's over. Now you need to go crawl back in your little shed. Peter doesn't want you anymore."

"Garrett, don't do this," she pleaded. "I need to talk to Peter. He would never break up this way. He's better than that."

"Listen up. You have no idea how important he is in this industry. He has far more meaningful things to do than run off to you all the time. You're holding him back. You were lucky to know him at all."

Her nerves were at a breaking point. One more strain would split the thread, and she would unravel. If what Garrett said was true, she'd never speak to Peter again. He was right; she was lucky to have known Peter. He changed her world for the better. She prayed Garrett was wrong, but what if he wasn't? Tears rolled down her face. She tried to hold herself together. If Peter wanted to break up, she didn't want to be the girl who begged and never let go. He'd been so good to her, and he deserved better.

"Do me one favor?" she asked.

"I told you, he doesn't want to talk to you."

"I know, just give him a message, please," Libby pleaded again as she hid next to the barn behind the house.

"What?" he answered flatly.

She swiped the tears with her arm.

"Tell him . . ." She paused, trying to find the right words. "Tell him, he saved me. And that it's okay, I get it." She knew it sounded stupid, but it was the truth. He'd saved her from the depths of depression. Tears poured down her face. She swiped her arm across her nose. She never expected she and Peter would last forever, but how could he end it like this?

Garrett stayed silent on the other end.

"Garrett? Please tell him for me. Please." She sobbed, gulping for breath.

"Yeah, whatever. I gotta go."

The phone clicked dead.

She wanted to call back but knew Garrett wouldn't put her through. She leaned against the side of the barn and covered her face with her hands. A tidal wave of anguish crashed over her. She slid into the tall grass, and sobs of grief escaped. She shouldn't have assumed a life with Peter could be real. It was a fantasy now ripped apart. Life couldn't possibly get any worse.

15

Peter slid his room key in the door, and a soft click and a green light appeared. He let himself in the hotel suite to find Garrett alone with a satisfied smirk on his face.

"What's up?" Peter asked.

"Taking care of some business." Garrett stared at Peter and didn't look away.

Peter looked around the cluttered desk and dresser. "Have you seen my phone? I thought it was in my coat, but I can't find it and I need to call Libby."

"It's probably on the bus."

"Yeah, maybe." Something about Garrett seemed odd, but Peter brushed it off.

• • •

Libby was huddled against the barn, huge gulping breaths racking her body. Locked in her private misery, she didn't hear Aunt Marge approach.

"What are you doing out here?" Aunt Marge held a shotgun in the crook of her arm.

Libby looked up from the frozen ground. Her lower lip shook as her tear-filled eyes rested on the weapon. What was Aunt Marge doing with a shotgun?

"Speak up." Her aunt's piercing words brought Libby back around. "You should be on the bus to school, not lurking around my barn. What are you looking for?" Aunt Marge's eyes narrowed. "What did you see?"

"Peter broke up with me," she uttered, her voice breaking. A new onslaught of tears and hiccups erupted.

"Good. Now maybe you'll pay attention when I tell you something. He was a snooping rich boy nosing around where he didn't belong. I knew this would happen. You're too damned stubborn to listen to me. You think you know everything. Well, I'll tell you, little Miss Know-It-All, you haven't got a clue about life."

Libby barely listened as her angry aunt ranted. Her words meant nothing. Without Peter, her world was empty. Tears overflowed anew.

"Now move your lazy ass up off the ground and get to school. I have work to do and you're interfering." She waved the gun in the direction of the road.

Libby fumbled with her book bag and rose, her body trembling with emotion. "I missed the bus."

Aunt Marge looked her up and down. "That was stupid.

Looks like you'll have a long walk to think about how to avoid that mistake again."

Libby's eyes widened. "It's five miles."

Aunt Marge shrugged. "Then you better get started." Aunt Marge stood steadfast like the vacant farm buildings, ugly after years of neglect. Would Libby turn out the same way?

This confrontation was more than she could handle. Libby gulped. No option but to go. Resigned, she walked around the dilapidated barn; the wide door hung open on rusted hinges. She automatically glanced inside.

Libby shouldn't have been surprised at what she saw.

She couldn't turn away from dozens of small plastic bags that sat in tidy rows. She stepped into the barn. Piles of dried plants and weight scales filled a table. Grow lights shone over large green plants. *Marijuana.*

She turned to face her aunt and laughed at the irony. The woman who restricted Libby's every move in the guise of good behavior was growing pot!

Rage etched Aunt Marge's haggard face. "You think you're so smart. Well, you're an ignorant, self-absorbed child." She stalked closer. "How long ago did your weak, spineless father dump you here? A year? More? And you finally get curious? You're as brainless as your idiot mother."

"Don't talk about my mother like that! She was amazing!" Anger replaced her sorrow.

"Your mother was a fool. She never accomplished a

damned thing in her life. She spent years raising you and your bratty sister, and for what? To get splattered on the highway like a bug? Not much of a life."

The cruel words horrified Libby. "How dare you. You . . . you bitch!"

"Watch your mouth, little girl. I'm all you've got left in this world, and you'd be ill advised to screw this up, too."

Libby bit back her words. Things were happening too fast. She needed to tread carefully and sort things out. She stepped back, away from her aunt, away from the pot. Without another word, she turned toward the road.

"That's more like it. Get yourself to school, and if you know what's good for you, you'll keep your mouth shut."

Libby started her long trek down the country road, glad to escape her aunt's insanity. The pea gravel crunched under each step like the touch of sandpaper rubbing her raw nerves. After a while, the sound became a soothing anthem, lulling her distraught mind into a murky haze, where she could rehash the happenings of this morning in a distant, detached way.

Mile after mile she walked, oblivious to the occasional car speeding by. When Mom and Sarah died, she'd been in shock. This was different. Their deaths were tragic, horrible accidents. Today, the people ripping her life apart knew what they were doing. It emotionally exhausted her. She was tired of being nice, tired of doing what people told her, tired of being let down. Aunt Marge's words stung. There was no one left for Libby, and she refused to think of her aunt as a guardian. The woman was a monster. How could her dad leave her with this lunatic?

A car passed her, slowed, then pulled over and stopped. Libby plodded forward, eventually reaching it.

"Libby, is that you?" Miss Orman leaned across the front seat and peeked out the open passenger window.

Libby stopped next to the window.

"Why are you walking? Get in." Miss Orman reached across to open the door.

"It's been a bad morning." Libby climbed into the car and set her pack on the floor. Her left hand still gripped her phone.

Ms. Orman took in Libby's disheveled appearance. "Are you okay?"

Libby nodded, but her blank expression remained. She knew her tearstained face was all blotchy. She stared down at the dirt on her secondhand coat and threadbare jeans.

"Do you want to tell me what happened?"

Libby shook her head and stared straight ahead, feeling as fragile as a porcelain dish. Miss Orman checked for traffic and pulled back onto the road.

After a minute, Libby spoke. "My aunt is growing and selling pot."

Ms. Orman's head snapped to look at her. "What did you say?"

"She keeps it in the barn. I saw it this morning. I always

wondered why she spent so much time out there." Libby didn't know why she told her. It just came out. It didn't really matter anymore. Nothing did.

"Oh dear God. I knew your aunt was odd, but I never suspected her of being a drug dealer."

"Peter broke up with me," Libby said in a monotone voice she barely recognized and held her phone up as confirmation.

"I'm so sorry." Miss Orman reached across and patted Libby's arm. "I wish I could protect you from the painful realities of life."

"It's okay, I'm used to people leaving." Everyone left. Her mom and sister died. Her dad abandoned her in Rockville. And now Peter. She never deserved him anyway.

"This is going to be okay. I promise. Someday you'll look back and this will be a small blip in your life. You'll be happy and successful, and no one will hold you back from great things."

Libby didn't respond.

"Listen, I'm going to help you through this. I'm leaving town for Thanksgiving weekend with my fiancé, but as soon as I get back, we're going to make all this ugliness go away. I promise. Okay?" Miss Orman waited for Libby to react, as though she needed reassurance herself.

"Okay," Libby said, her voice dull as they pulled into the school parking lot.

"Why don't you come to my office, and we can talk for

a while or have a little something to eat? You look like you could use a good meal. When's the last time you ate?"

"I'd rather just go to class." She was already out the door, her backpack hanging heavy on her weary shoulders.

"All right, but I'm here for you, whatever you need," Miss Orman said as Libby disappeared into the mass of students.

• • •

Later that day, Peter stood in the hotel suite exhausted from a long day packed with interviews. In his palm lay the pieces of his broken phone. "Garrett, what the hell is this?"

"What are you doing messing with my stuff?" Garrett's face turned red and pinched.

"I couldn't find my phone, so I was looking for yours so I could call Libby, but I found mine instead. What gives?"

"Oh yeah, that. Well, ya see, your phone had a little accident. I didn't want to tell you, 'cause I know how you overreact whenever your little hottie is involved."

Peter tensed. Garrett was too cocky, even for him. Something was up. Whenever Garrett got like this it was because he'd screwed with other people's business. Guarded, Peter asked, "What happened?"

"Nothing, really." Garrett's beady eyes stared him down.

Peter knew his brother was lying. A bad feeling sat in the pit of his stomach. "You son of a bitch, what the hell did you do?"

"Actually, I did you a favor. In fact, you should thank me for cleaning up your mess. You won't have to deal with your Midwest farm girl anymore."

Peter dropped the broken pieces of the phone on the side table. He stalked across the room and grabbed Garrett by the front of his designer shirt and shook him. "You better start talking, and fast." He tightened his grip and lifted Garrett off his feet. Fabric ripped beneath his hands.

"Chill man, will ya? You're ruining my new shirt. See what I mean? One mention of your little girlfriend and you go postal."

Peter was about to respond when Adam walked in, futzing with his camera. He took one look at Peter and Garrett. "Dude, what are you doing? Mom and Dad are, like, ten feet away."

Peter shoved Garrett away, disgusted, but his piercing glare remained. Garrett shrugged and fixed his collar back in place.

"Jeez, what'd you do to piss off Peter? Hit on his girlfriend or something?" Adam plopped onto the couch between the two.

"Adam, shut it," Peter said through clenched teeth.

"More like 'something.'" Garrett puffed up his chest.

"Oh, I gotta hear this." Adam put his feet up on the couch and grinned, with his camera at the ready.

"Peter's little stalker friend won't be bothering him anymore. Turns out she got dumped today." Garrett crossed his arms, looking satisfied with himself. Peter's heart clenched.

Adam lowered his camera, confusion on his face. "Peter, you dumped Libby?"

Peter spoke slowly, his words measured and jaw clenched. "No, I haven't talked to Libby today. My phone has been missing. Garrett, you better tell me what you did right now, or so help me, I'll break your frickin' neck." He forced his fisted hands to his sides, not trusting himself.

"This morning, while you were on your run, I gave your little friend a call." Garrett loved an audience, even if it was only Adam. "I told her how bored you are with her and that you want her to go away. Forever." Garrett raised an eyebrow, an open challenge to Peter.

Adam's eyes grew wide with shock. "Garrett, you're a dead man."

"Peter doesn't have it in him. Plus, he'd rather go write a song about it."

Hot rage overcame Peter. "You're lying. You wouldn't dare call Libby."

"I did more than dare. I was quite convincing. I even had the phone company cancel her service!"

Peter dove across the coffee table and sent a flower arrangement crashing to the floor. He slammed into Garrett and knocked the breath out of him as they hit the floor. They rolled around on the hardwood as Peter struck out and tried to pin his brother down. Garrett plowed into an antique side table, knocking it over along with a crystal lamp that shattered on impact.

Deaf to everything other than his malicious brother, Peter heaved each breath. He grabbed Garrett by the shoulders and slammed him against the floor. A loud thud sounded at the impact of his head to hardwood. Garrett was unable to avoid Peter's powerful blows any longer.

Peter pinned him and, blind with rage, delivered direct hits. His body hummed with an unseen drive. He noticed the taste of blood in his mouth from one lucky shot Garrett snuck through. But nothing mattered other than the fact Garrett had gone after Libby and hurt her. It was unforgiveable. She'd suffered too much, and this time it was by the hand of his egotistical, power-hungry brother.

Peter went for another hit when he felt himself yanked off the struggling Garrett. His dad and Roger did all they could to restrain him. His mom watched in horror.

"Peter, what the hell is going on in here? Are you out of your mind?" his father roared.

"Jett, calm down. It's not good for your heart," Peter's mom pleaded, taking his father by the arm.

Peter's breath came in quick, heavy bursts, as adrenaline coursed through his body. He resisted the urge to pummel Garrett into oblivion. The last thing he wanted was more heart problems for his dad. He shrugged away their grip.

"Karen, I'm fine." His father looked from Peter to Garrett, waiting for an answer. "Garrett, you want to explain why Peter felt the need to fight with you just minutes after a camera crew left the room?"

The sound of Adam's camera clicking filled the void. He lounged on the couch, not a care in the world. A carefree grin on his face, he snapped shots of the action, enjoying the drama.

"Adam, put that damned camera down! The last thing we need is evidence of this debacle," his father said.

Garrett lay on the floor, his carefully styled hair a mess, and the beginnings of a fat lip growing. "He's just a little bent out of shape that I called Libby and broke it off for him."

"You didn't!" His mom turned on Garrett in disbelief. "What is wrong with you!"

"I don't know why you're surprised. Garrett always does whatever serves him best. He's jealous whenever I have something he doesn't," Peter yelled.

"Bull! Someone had to end your little-boy crush." Garrett looked around at their parents, Adam, and Roger. "Come on, it's not like we haven't talked about how messed up Peter's been ever since he started going out with her." Garrett stood up, his torn shirt untucked and wrinkled, a bruise beginning to form under his eye. "I'm just the one with the guts to follow through." Garrett touched his swollen lip and flinched.

Peter couldn't believe what he heard. "You've been talking about my relationship with Libby?" He pushed his hair back in frustration.

"Heck, Dad even agreed. He said the band would be better off if you lost the deadweight."

"Garrett, that's enough." His father's voice was stern, but Peter noticed his guilty eyes.

He turned to his dad. "How could you do this to us, to me?"

"Peter, calm down," his dad ordered condescendingly. Yet he wouldn't look him in the eye.

"No, I'm not going to calm down!" Peter yelled. "You let Garrett do this! You cut us off!" Of all the manipulative things Garrett had done over the years, this was by far the worst. His family was interfering in his life. He couldn't believe they would turn against him. They'd crossed the line.

"This little thing with you two has gone on long enough. It's time to get serious with your music. We have a lot coming up," his father said.

"What do you mean it's gone on long enough? You're putting a timetable on my relationships?"

"It was hardly a relationship, son. You're young. You'll date lots of girls."

"I don't want lots of girls, I want Libby. And YES, it IS a relationship. She gets me. She doesn't care about all this."

He waved his hands around at the fancy trappings of the room. "And since when am I not serious about my music? Don't you dare use that as an excuse! We've never been as good or successful as we are now."

"That's right, and now you boys have the chance to take this thing to the next level. You don't need any distractions."

"Oh, and Garrett's booty calls after every show aren't a distraction?" Peter accused.

His mother shot a surprised and disappointed look at Garrett. She shook her head. "We'll deal with you later."

"What? The ladies love me," Garrett bragged.

"My God, Dad! Libby's not a distraction, she's my sanity." He'd been happier these past couple months than ever before.

"You have your family for sanity. That's going to have to be good enough," his dad said, pointing a finger at him.

"Are you kidding me? This family is pushing me over the edge! I'm surrounded by you day and night." Peter paced in the small area. "If we're not holed up in a recording studio, we're on that damned bus. I never get a moment to myself, a private phone conversation, or a chance to write without someone interrupting or sticking in their two cents!"

"Peter, that's enough." His mother stepped in, trying to soothe his anger.

He let out a deep sigh. "I love her, Mom." He looked from his dad, who stepped away and rolled his eyes, and then to his mom, who offered a look of compassion.

"Honey, she isn't what she seems." She placed a hand on his shoulder.

"What are you talking about?" He shrugged her hand away.

"Libby's mother has a police record," she said.

"What?" He shook his head. "No, no! She doesn't." He couldn't believe what he was hearing. Where was this coming from, and why would his mother repeat such a horrible lie?

"Peter, Roger has a copy of the police record to prove it."

"What? You had her investigated?"

"Well, you were spending all your free time talking to her or going to see her. We've never met the girl. Even your brother thought the situation was a bit odd," she confessed.

Peter looked at his brothers. Adam enjoyed the family drama, and Garrett sported a cocky look of superiority. "Since when do you listen to Garrett? He's only doing this because he can't stand to see me happy."

He turned back to his mother. "You're wrong about Libby's mother."

His parents exchanged a worried glance.

Peter needed them to understand and to know the truth about Libby. "Her mother's dead. She died in a car accident a couple years ago. So she can't have a police record. That's why Libby's living in Rockville with her aunt. Libby isn't even from Wisconsin."

His mother looked at him with sympathy. "She's told you some tall tales. She wanted you to like her. I'm sure she didn't mean to hurt you."

"You're not listening, either one of you! Libby's entire family was in the car. Her little sister died that day, too. Libby's got scars to prove it. After the funeral, her dad lost it, and she got dumped at her aunt's. It's not her fault if her aunt's a criminal. My God!" He threw his hands in the air, frustrated beyond belief. He looked to each family member, willing them to understand. The regret on his mother's face told him she now understood.

"Roger got it wrong. Mom, you never should have let this happen." Peter shook his head, walked over to his mother, and spoke quietly. "I need to talk to her. I need to fix this. I can't imagine what she's thinking. I don't even know how to get ahold of her without going to Rockville."

"No one's going anywhere," his father interrupted, crossing his arms. "We're headed home to San Antonio tonight for Thanksgiving tomorrow. Plus, the European tour is about to kick off, and we're already behind schedule with promotion."

His mom rubbed his back. "Don't worry, we'll get ahold of her. It'll be all right. I know it seems terrible right now, but you'll feel better tomorrow."

"No, I won't feel better until I can talk to her and make

sure she knows we're okay." Thank God Mom understood. He could always count on her in a crisis.

• • •

That night, Libby, wearing a baggy T-shirt, paced her bedroom, unable to sleep. She didn't want to be at school, and now she didn't want to be here, either. When she came home, Aunt Marge gave her the silent treatment, which was fine. The acrid stench of pot filled the air. A bag of marijuana sat on the kitchen counter like a huge elephant in the room. Libby supposed now that Aunt Marge's business dealings were out in the open, she didn't feel the need to hide anything anymore.

The evening inched by, a slow torture into night. More than anything, Libby wanted Peter. She didn't care what Garrett said. In her eyes, Peter would always be perfect. She would love him for the rest of her life.

She broke down and tried to call him, in desperate hope that Garrett was wrong, but her phone had no connection. Garrett had cut the phone service and, as a result, cut Libby out of Peter's life. It was over. This flashy phone was no more than an empty shell.

Her stomach growled with hunger, but she didn't dare go downstairs in search of food. She didn't trust herself around Aunt Marge. What she really wanted to do was light the barn on fire and watch her aunt flip out as she lost the only thing she cared about go up in smoke.

Libby plopped back down on the bed, miserable, wishing she could sleep. It was after 11:00 p.m., and her body wouldn't give in. Some freakish adrenaline from losing Peter consumed her body. She stared at the shadows the moonlight cast across her room. She tried to block out all the painful memories. Her mom covered in shattered glass. Her sister hooked up to machines that couldn't save her. Her big, strong father crumbling before her eyes. His car driving away. The memories morphed into equally painful thoughts of Peter; him, singing to her at Parfrey's Glen, the way he held her in his arms, and his eyes gazing deep into hers.

Suddenly, a crash sounded downstairs. She jerked up in bed and heard another crash, then loud voices yelling. She sat paralyzed on her bed, unsure what to do. Downstairs, her aunt's shrieks filled the house.

Someone was breaking into the house.

16

Footsteps pounded up the stairs and paralysis turned to action. Libby leapt off the bed, searching the room for a safe hiding place. The closet held almost nothing and wouldn't conceal her; the furniture was sparse with nothing to hide behind. In unbearable panic, she ran to the bed and began to crawl under it, smacking her chin on the floor and scraping her shoulder against the ancient frame.

Her bedroom door burst open and two enormous men rushed in. Their bright flashlights caught her attempt at escape.

Her heart nearly exploded as she clawed to fit under the bed. They were on her in an instant. Rough hands dragged her back out, causing her nightshirt to slide up and reveal her bare legs and underwear.

"No!" she screamed at the top of her lungs, hoping to

alert someone, anyone to help. She dug her fingernails into the threadbare carpet, and kicked out at her attackers. Pure terror consumed her.

Libby fought them with a strength she never knew she possessed. A heavy boot slammed into her back, knocked the wind out of her, and pinned her to the floor. Her heart pounded huge, loud thunks. Tears streaked her face in defeat. As she struggled to breathe, the men flipped her over and blinded her with their bright flashlights.

"Jesus, Smith, she's a kid," one of the attackers said.

"Like that makes a difference," the other responded.

"Back off. Let her breathe," the first voice said.

A set of hands moved away, but the other kept her locked in an iron grip. The lights left her face and moved expertly throughout the room.

"This room's clear, just the girl," an annoyed voice called.

In the moonlit room, she saw the shadowed men look at each other and share an unspoken thought. They hauled her to her feet, and before she could react, cold smooth metal clicked tight around her wrist. Her arm was pulled to the head of her bed where the other end clicked around the wrought-iron bar.

Dumbfounded, she looked at her wrist and back at the men. *What the hell?*

"To keep you from running off." The dark man answered her unspoken question.

Simultaneously, the two giants turned and left her

room. Large white letters were printed on the back of their coats.

SWAT

Relief and dread washed over her as she struggled to take a deep breath. They weren't here to attack her; they were here for the pot. She moved her arm and found it securely locked to the bed. Did they suspect her? With her luck, Aunt Marge would pin the drugs on her. The kids at school would love this.

Miss Orman must have reported it. It was stupid to have told her. Libby paused. Why should she want to protect Aunt Marge? She was a hideous person who deserved what she got. Libby no longer heard her aunt's screeching, but could imagine her going ballistic. A tiny smile lit her face.

As Libby's pulse slowed to a healthier pace, she noticed more men lurking outside, covertly checking all the outbuildings as if they were on a police detective show. The moonlight illuminated the yard, revealing how they used hand signals as they rushed from building to building. As the minutes passed, their urgency slowed and lights began to appear in the barn.

Libby grinned. Aunt Marge was going down.

Unable to do much else, Libby watched from her window as the SWAT team took pictures and started moving the contents of the barn. Had they forgotten about her? It seemed like hours had passed, but it might have only been minutes. She looked out across the fields to Parfrey's Glen, at one time her sanctuary, and then, after meeting Peter, her haven. Would he ever stop there again? No, probably not. She sat on the edge of the bed, head low. Why did life have to suck so much?

A few minutes later, a woman startled her when she walked into the room. Libby never heard her on the stairs.

"Hi, I'm Officer Decker and I'm going to take you downstairs to ask you some questions. Do you understand?" She stood as formidable as a giant oak.

"Yes, ma'am," Libby answered.

"Stand up, please. I'm going to move this cuff from the bed to your other wrist."

"Please don't do that. I didn't do anything wrong. Honest," Libby implored, but obeyed her instruction.

"It's policy. Until you've been released from suspicion, we need to take precautions."

• • •

Libby sat in the back of a squad car. She had never wondered what getting arrested would be like, but now the experience was forever ingrained in her mind. She absorbed the view of massive equipment in the front of the car. The equipment seemed more useful to fly a jet plane than track down small-town drug dealers.

Officer Decker turned down the volume on the police radio, but it still squawked in the background. Tiny red and yellow lights lit the console. A strong scent permeated the vehicle, a combination of leather, plastic, and unknown smells she'd rather not guess at. She sank back into the seat, miserable.

"Thanks for your patience, Libby. I know this has been a long night." Officer Decker's demeanor changed now that the authorities knew she had nothing to do with Aunt Marge's pot selling. "Are you sure there isn't anyone we can call for you? A friend or neighbor?"

"Nope. No one." Her only friend was Peter, and he had disconnected himself from her life. What would she say if she could get through to him? *Hi, you don't want to be with me anymore, but can you save me from my train wreck of a life?*

"Anyone at school?" Officer Decker was reaching for someone, anyone to call, but the fact was, no one existed. Just her dad, and they already knew he'd deserted her.

"There is one person," Libby started. Officer Decker's eyes lit, her pad open and pen ready. "My school counselor, Miss Orman, but she's out of town for Thanksgiving weekend."

"I see." The officer appeared disappointed as she closed the pad. Why would she care if Libby had no friends?

"Can I go back inside now?" Despite all the adrenaline from earlier, Libby felt exhausted. She wanted to collapse into bed and put this awful episode behind her.

"I'm afraid that's not possible. This is a crime scene and it will be investigated for the next few days, maybe longer."

"Where am I supposed to go?" Libby sat up and peeked through the wire divider protecting the officer from the dangerous suspects trapped in the backseat.

"That's what I've been trying to determine. You're too old for foster care." The officer seemed disappointed.

"Foster care! What are you talking about? I'm almost seventeen. I can take care of myself. All I need is a place to stay until I can get back in the house." There was no way they were putting her in some foster home. The only things she ever heard about foster homes were stories about weird people who took in kids for the state money, and the kids were often abused.

"Calm down," the officer interrupted. "As I said, you're too old. Foster care is designed for younger kids, not older teens."

"How soon until my aunt is out? I'll be fine until she posts bail or whatever she needs to do." Libby didn't know how she'd come up with money to post bail and could barely believe she was now lobbying to stay with her aunt. What a strange twist of fate. Now maybe Aunt Marge needed her. How long should she let her sit locked up before helping her out?

"I'm afraid your aunt will be tied up in the legal system for quite some time. In addition to growing marijuana with intent to deliver, which is a felony crime, she will likely be charged with child neglect and contributing to the delinquency of a minor."

"Child neglect? Delinquency of a minor? Come on, I'm fine." A sense of dread choked her.

"Look at where you're sitting right now. A responsible adult would not have put you in this situation." Officer Decker pierced her with a knowing look. Libby slumped against the seat, temporarily out of words to argue.

The officer turned forward, picked up her radio, and clicked the side button. "Officer Decker at number 4319 County Road T. Need Dell County Social Services for system placement of a sixteen-year-old female."

The radio crackled. "Local placement isn't possible until after the holiday weekend. You'll be looking at transfer placement to a group home in Milwaukee County."

Libby shot forward, grabbing the metal divider that kept her from the horrible radio. "What do you mean 'group home'?" She gripped the thick metal and shook it to get the officer's attention. "You can't send me to a group home. Please, I can't go there." Her dread exploded into full-scale panic. Bad things happened at those places.

"Headquarters, I'll call social services direct from a private line." The officer glanced at Libby as she spoke, then replaced the radio piece to the console.

"Please listen. My dad needs to know where I am. If I'm not here, he won't know how to find me." She rattled the divider, wanting to crawl through to the other side and knock sense into the stubborn woman.

"I'm sorry, but there's no other way. You said yourself there isn't anyone else to step in. No family, no neighbors, no friends. You'll be fine," she said in a tone that told Libby she didn't believe her own words. "Sit tight. I'll be back after finishing up your transfer arrangements." She opened the door to the patrol car.

"Wait! Don't go." She needed to convince the officer to let her stay at the farmhouse. She couldn't let them send her away.

Officer Decker offered a strained smile but exited the car, shutting the door firmly. Libby pounded on the metal divider like a criminal gone berserk. She'd imagined she'd live with her aunt until graduation or until her dad came back. This was beyond horrible. Her life was spinning into a total disaster. How could her dad leave her to this?

17

"**Pass** the gravy, would ya, buddy?" Peter said to his young cousin Ryan.

They'd gathered around the Thanksgiving table with the large extended family. Peter couldn't stop wondering about Libby, stuck with her lunatic aunt. He doubted a turkey dinner was involved. All he could picture was her alone, thinking he dumped her. He tried to call her using another phone, but Garrett had canceled the cell service to her number. Now Peter had to wait until the next day to try and get Libby's service reinstated and to replace his phone.

"This one's empty." Ryan looked up at him with innocent eyes.

"Here, Peter. There's plenty in this bowl." Carly, his uncle Steve's stepdaughter, offered another bowl of steaming turkey gravy. She delivered a coy smile and all but batted her eyes. Peter pretended not to notice. He didn't want to encourage her.

Determined to bury his heartache over Libby, he stuffed himself with food. Usually, he loved Thanksgiving, but this year, the gathering of twenty people was more than he could handle. He took the bowl from Carly's eager hands. "Thanks." He forced a smile and ladled the rich gravy over his second helping of turkey, stuffing, and cheesy potato casserole, turning the contents on his plate into a thick stew.

"Where does he put all that food?" Grandma Jamieson commented, looking at his plate mounded with food. Peter smiled at Grandma and shoveled in another mouthful.

His mother looked at him warmly. "Ever since Peter turned fourteen, he's always eating, and he runs every day, so that boosts his appetite even more. It's near impossible to keep these boys fed."

Peter responded with a black look. He didn't feel like making nice with his family. They were a bunch of traitors.

"I can't imagine your grocery bill," Becky, Uncle Steve's new wife, commented. "My Carly eats like a little bird. I swear some days I have to remind her to eat." Aunt Becky bragged about her daughter's ultra-skinny body. The girl wore her clothes so tight, they left little to the imagination. Carly took a tiny bite of green bean and feigned embarrassment.

"Now that we've inhaled most of this meal, who wants to start with their thanks?" his mom asked. Every year she forced them to participate in this ritual. Peter and his brothers groaned.

His mother eyed them. "Boys, you disappoint me. This year, more than any other, we have so much to be thankful for."

Peter scraped potatoes from the side of his plate and stuffed his mouth. He looked directly at his mother and shrugged.

"Fine. I'll start." She wiped the corners of her mouth with a linen napkin, then set it aside. "I am thankful for the amazing doctors and medical staff at Cedars-Sinai." She reached out and took her husband's hand. "Without their dedication and talent, I might have lost you." She gazed at his dad; tears welled in her eyes.

"And I thought you were going to say you were thankful to get a few days freedom while I was in the hospital," his father said. His mother shot him a wry expression.

Each person in turn offered up something to be thankful for. Next came Garrett.

"I'm thankful Peter's got such a weak left hook." He rubbed his bruised cheekbone for effect.

Their mother pierced Garrett with a powerful stare. Carly looked from Peter to Garrett and back again, intrigued. Peter set his fork down, his jaw clenched. He'd love to slug him again. The asshole deserved it and much more.

"What are you thankful for, Peter?" Grandma asked, oblivious to the tension between the two brothers.

Peter looked from Garrett to his father and mother. "Absolutely nothing." He controlled his anger. He didn't want to upset Grandma.

"Peter," his father warned. "We all have something to be thankful for. Try that again."

Inside he fumed. He was thankful to have Libby, but then Garrett derailed that. All he could think about was his need to talk to her and clear everything up. He wanted Libby with him. Other than that, he only felt anger—anger at his family's interference, at being stuck in this fake happy holiday celebration, and at the clueless girl sitting next to him, starstruck over his every word like a rabid fan.

All eyes focused on him, including his father's.

"All right. What am I thankful for? Let's see. I could say our sold-out tour or our platinum album, but no, that's pretty shallow." He gave a pointed look at each of his brothers and his parents. He thought of Libby and how alone she must feel. "I'm thankful to have a family I can be mad at. Even though they make my life a living hell, at least they exist." His words were clipped and short. "Because if I didn't have a family, I'd be all alone in the world. Can you imagine how lonely and difficult life would be if I didn't have Mom always hovering or Dad caring enough to help us achieve our dreams, or brothers to piss off and fight with?"

Peter set a defiant stare at his parents, driving home the sad reality of Libby's life. His mother looked down at her plate.

"That's enough," his father said. A silent void filled the room as the relatives shared uncomfortable looks. "Why don't you make yourself useful? There are a lot of dishes on this table that need washing. Perhaps that'll help clear your head."

The guests watched the awkward battle. His young cousins looked confused.

"Fine with me." Peter shoved back from the table, grabbed his dishes, and went to the kitchen.

"I'll help." Carly popped up and chased after him.

• • •

Peter's waterlogged hands sank deep into their third round of dishes. Despite his pleas to be left alone, Carly stuck with him and dried every dish. Stacks of clean, dried china and silverware lay as evidence of their work.

"What did I do to make you hate me?" She leaned against the kitchen counter, an irritated expression on her face.

"Huh?" Peter looked up from the dishwater.

"I've been trying to talk to you all day, and you treat me like I'm diseased. What'd I ever do to you?" She folded her arms across her chest, the damp dish towel in hand.

"Nothing. Sorry. I've just got a lot on my mind." He

turned back to his sulking and dunked another serving bowl.

"Guys can be such jerks. Steve said you were really nice, but I think he must have been talking about Garrett."

Peter's head snapped around, and he eyed her smug expression. "That's a good one." He fought the smile that threatened. She had saved him a ton of work by helping out. The least he could do was be nice.

"What's got you so pissed?" she asked, twirling her dish towel.

Peter glanced at her, an eyebrow raised.

"Hello, you've been brooding all day and your little speech in there just proves you've got major attitude. You're mad you got stuck with family all day?"

"I'm stuck with family every day. Today's better than most. With more people around, it helps distract them." He rinsed another platter and placed it with the mounting pile of china stacked in the drainer. "You're falling behind." He pointed to the waiting dishes.

Carly glared at him, then resumed her chore. After that, Peter finally allowed himself a smile. He found it easier to be nice to Carly. As Peter refilled the sink, Carly placed another plate with the huge pile of clean dishes on the island counter.

"God, there's a lot of dishes. Your dad is nasty to make you do all this."

"Yeah, Jett's real good at doling out punishment."

"What do you do for fun around here?" Carly asked.

"Oh, I don't know." With the faucet on, Peter suddenly grabbed the spray hose and turned it on her. Carly shrieked in surprise and tried to block his water assault with the platter in her hands. He shot the spray across the room as she tried to dodge it. By the time they were done, both were laughing from the water fight and Carly's skilled towel snapping. He ended up having a good time despite himself.

• • •

After that, the day improved. He played cards with his brothers and cousins.

"Take that!" Peter slapped his last card on the pile and won the hand.

Carly sat next to him, clinging to his every word. She glowed each time Peter looked her way. He knew he shouldn't encourage her, but it felt good to laugh and have fun for just a little while.

"Ready for pie?" his mom asked. Hungry voices cheered. "It's ready in the kitchen. You can join the adults in the living room."

The mob of kids bustled past; Peter and Carly shared a joke as they walked by.

A few minutes later, everyone sat in the great room. The room overflowed with comfortable furniture and oversized potted plants; a baby grand stood in one corner. He and his brothers often used the room to practice or just sit and play whatever instrument they were in the mood for. On one side of the room, Adam's camera sat on a tripod waiting for the traditional family photos.

"Peter, would you play something for me? It's been so long," Grandma Jamieson asked.

"Sure, Grandma," Peter said from his seat next to Carly. He stood and placed his empty plate on the coffee table. He flexed his fingers. Carly smiled, clearly excited to see him perform. He wasn't really sure what to do with that.

Peter sat behind the piano. "What would you like to hear, Grandma?"

"How about something new? Are you working on anything?"

"Mom, Peter is always working on something new. He can't seem to turn his writing off." His parents shared a proud look. He ignored them.

"All right, play something pretty for me," Grandma said.

Peter rewarded her with a loving smile. The two of them always shared a special connection. He remembered the story about when his mom was in the hospital delivering Adam several weeks too early. While Adam stayed in the hospital for more than a week, his grandparents took care of him and Garrett. During that time, five-year-old Garrett watched television and played outside with neighbor kids. But Peter stuck by his grandmother's side. If she worked in her flower beds, three-year-old Peter was with her. When she made beds, he tried to help. He insisted that Grandma teach him to play the aging upright piano in the living room. A few days later when his parents picked him up, he had already mastered "Twinkle, Twinkle, Little Star."

Peter drew in a breath and released it, then began to play. At first, his fingers barely touched the keys. A beautiful melody rose from the piano. The room quieted as he artfully mastered the instrument.

He became one with the music. His body moved gently as he played, lost to the world around him. The tender piece filled the air with its beauty and the loving way he performed.

"This sounds familiar, but I can't place it," he heard his mom comment.

Pride beamed on his grandmother's face. He smiled at her. Carly sat alone on the love seat, with a look of awe.

"Mom," Adam spoke up. "It's the song he wrote about Libby, 'Angel Kisses.'"

And then sadness filled his heart again. The energy of the music intensified as the angst of the tune built, and Peter laid bare his broken heart. One thing he'd learned over the years is that music is what feelings sound like. And his feelings were all about Libby.

The beautiful piece slowed and returned to the beginning melody. Peter's emotion filled the room. He was a master at moving an audience. When his long fingers struck the final chord, his head dropped to his chest. First, the room echoed in silence, and then burst with applause.

Peter reached up and brushed away a single tear. He missed Libby so much. And then he heard his mom speak to his dad.

"Jett, maybe it wouldn't hurt to get Peter together with Libby for just a day before we leave for Europe."

"I suppose. If it lifts this depression he's in, fine," his dad gave in.

One glance at Carly and he saw her face fall with disappointment as she realized his heart belonged to someone else.

18

Three weeks later, Libby stepped quietly through the door of the Milwaukee group home. Could she be lucky enough that her housemates would be asleep?

"You bring me anything good?" Michael, a tall, skinny kid, asked from the couch where he lay watching some show featuring monster trucks.

"This is all they had left." She tossed him a white takeout bag. "Maybe there'll be extras from the fish fry tomorrow."

Days after arriving at the group home, Libby got a job working at a restaurant in the mall. If she was going to be stuck living in this hellhole, she planned to avoid it as much as possible. Only a few weeks had passed since her arrival on Thanksgiving Day. It felt like months.

"Damn, this is great, but where's my rings?" Michael stuffed a handful of fries in his mouth. He ate constantly, but was the skinniest guy she'd ever seen. The first time she'd laid eyes on him, she'd been terrified of his tattoos and piercings. Now she knew his image was mostly an act, probably for survival's sake. He looked tough but was harmless. He was also the closest thing she had to a friend here.

"Sorry, no onion rings tonight. Maybe next time." In an effort to blend in and not make enemies, Libby always brought back leftovers from the mall restaurant where she worked.

She walked down the hallway; her grip on her handbag tightened like a vise as she approached the girls' bedroom. Silently, she opened the door to the room she shared with Sophie, a volatile psychopath, who for some reason was determined to terrorize Libby, and Kelly, a pale girl who dyed her hair a deep black, wore dark eye makeup, and rarely spoke. Sophie sat on her messy bedsheets cleaning her fingernails with a jackknife as she rocked to her iPod. Kelly slept soundly in her depressed state.

Ignoring Sophie, Libby went straight to her side of the room and grabbed her shower stuff. Living at the home was a cross between a college dorm and juvenile hall. You kept your stuff to yourself. You didn't share, and stealing was a common occurrence. Libby's things disappeared on a regular basis. Within hours of her arrival on Thanksgiving Day, the phone Peter gave her disappeared. Her last tie to him had been permanently cut. She'd bet money Sophie was the klepto. Libby kept her money with her everywhere she went now, including the bathroom.

She grabbed a long T-shirt to sleep in, a robe, and padded to the door. A *swish* and then *thud* rang in her ear. Libby froze. Sophie's knife stuck in the wall just inches from her face. She held her breath, afraid to turn around.

"Hey, blondie, what's the big hurry? Aren't ya gonna say hi?" Sophie lounged against the headboard, a snarl on her face.

Libby ran out of the room. At least she knew the knife was in the wall and couldn't hurt her. Sophie's cruel laughter followed her.

Inside the bathroom, Libby locked the door and rested her head against it. Her hand gripped the doorknob until she could breathe again. She hated that girl. Her mom always said it was wrong to hate, that everyone had good in them. But her mom never met Sophie.

She closed the lid to the toilet and sat down and took a few moments to pull herself together, but it was getting harder. It took Libby every ounce of energy she possessed just to survive.

Scott, the leader of the group home, was nice enough, but he didn't have a clue what went on. Why a pacifist wanted a job surrounded by teenage derelicts, she couldn't imagine. His easygoing manner kept the kids a little less stressed, but he did a lousy job with behavior management.

She looked around the small bathroom. In here, she was safe from hassle, in the only spot she could be alone.

Before she took her shower, she grabbed cleaning supplies from under the sink and gave the room a quick once over. Everything in her world was a mess. At least she could shower in a bathroom that didn't have smears on the mirror and hair all over the sink. In a couple of minutes, the bathroom countertop and mirror were clean and smelled like lemons.

Libby inhaled deeply and released some of her stress. She turned on the shower and organized her stuff, pretending this was her own private place that no one would invade. After folding her work clothes, she stepped under the weak shower pressure and let warm water roll over her body. She tried to imagine she was in a magical place under a waterfall instead of this nightmarish prison.

She stood under the flow long after she was clean, wishing she could wash away the reality of her world. Her thoughts turned to Peter; she missed him so much. At least she didn't cry each time she thought of him anymore. She tried to call him from the group home phone as soon as she arrived. She needed to make sure Garrett wasn't pulling a cruel joke, but Peter didn't pick up and a recording said his voice mailbox was full. She even called his record company, but couldn't get past the operator. Peter was now a part of her past, like every other happy part of life. No knight in shining armor for Libby.

The water turned cool. She stepped out and dressed for bed. With wet hair hanging down her back and her arms filled, she left the security of the bathroom.

Halfway down the hall, a door opened and BJ, a teen-ager the size of a linebacker, stepped out and blocked her way.

Shit.

BJ looked more like thirty than seventeen. He scared the hell out of her.

"I thought I heard the shower going and hoped it was you. You're always up late, working hard. You need to relax. In fact, why don't you join me and I can help." He winked.

Libby bit the inside of her cheek. There was no good way to answer BJ, and there was no way she was stepping inside his room.

"What's the matter? You scared? You don't need to be scared of me. I'll be real gentle." BJ walked toward her, put his mammoth arms against the wall, and leaned over her. He took a lock of damp hair that hung over her shoulder and sniffed. "You smell real good. I could just eat you up."

Libby's stomach churned as she gripped her clothes and towel. She could turn around and run back to the bath-room. Or scream and hope Scott heard and would come to her rescue. But his room was on the other end of the house, and he slept to the hum of a fan.

Before she decided what to do, Michael sauntered down the hallway.

"Hey, guys, what's up? You having a party and didn't invite me?"

BJ glared at him, sending a message of cease and desist, but Michael ignored him.

"I'd love to join ya, but I need my beauty sleep. Now if you'll excuse me, I'll be on my way."

BJ stepped aside to let Michael pass. Michael pushed Libby ahead of him through the quick opening and toward her bedroom door before BJ realized what happened.

"Ladies first, don't you have some big test tomorrow or something? You shouldn't stay up so late," Michael said with a pointed look at Libby.

Libby quickly entered her shadowed bedroom and mouthed the words *thank you* so BJ wouldn't hear. Tomorrow, she'd bring onion rings home even if she had to pay for them herself.

The streetlight outside illuminated the room. Sophie slept on her back, her mouth open, as tunes from her iPod blared in her ears. Relieved, Libby put her stuff away and climbed into the lumpy bed.

Two close calls in one night; she wished she had the guts to run away, but there was nowhere to go. Michael told her plenty of kids ran away, and the authorities were too backlogged to care or go after them. She asked why kids stayed; he said most stayed either to pay their dues for their crimes or because it was a warm bed and three meals a day.

For Michael, she believed he lived a safer life here than on the streets.

She fell asleep wishing she and Peter had run away together when he first suggested it.

• • •

"Peter?"

"Yeah, Mom." He walked to the side of the stage, eager to avoid the sound check.

"Let's go talk in the dressing room."

Peter instantly knew it was about Libby. "What? You found her? Where is she?" His heart beat with excitement.

"It's a long story."

"Tell me," he said, desperate for news.

His mom glanced around. Peter followed her gaze. Adam and Garrett watched from their spots on stage. Crew members littered the arena, securing equipment and completing final security checks.

"I'm sorry. This is not the news I'd hoped to give." She gazed at him with love and sadness.

"What? What'd you find out?" Peter demanded.

"We tried to find her, but she's gone, honey. I'm so sorry."

"What do you mean gone? Gone where?" Peter didn't understand.

"We don't know." She tried to soothe him with words. "The authorities arrested her aunt for selling drugs. They couldn't locate Libby's father, so they placed her in foster care." His mom watched him closely. For once, his brothers stayed silent. Not a sound echoed in the arena as the crew looked on.

"How could they do that to her?" He shoved his hands through his hair and locked his fingers above his head, turning away to hide the anguish in his eyes.

"She tried to call you," she added.

Peter turned back to her, hoping for better news, as he fought back emotions. Please let it be with a message of where she was.

"Several times." His mom fumbled with some crumpled slips of paper. "The front office took these. They're dated a couple days after her aunt was arrested."

"And? What do they say?" He snatched them out of her hand.

"We called the number, Peter. It belonged to a pay phone at a mall in Milwaukee."

As the bad news continued, Peter stood paralyzed. His eyes became glassy as he read each message.

"Libby must have waited for hours. The last message said she was sorry." His mother spoke softly. "I can't imagine why. The poor girl never did anything wrong."

"Can they find her? There must be a record?" Peter's voice broke; he turned away, his chest heaving with each breath. He tried to hold back his emotions.

"We tried. They won't release the information. She's a

minor and under custody of the state. It's the law."

"This is shit!" he snapped, as his anger overpowered his pain. "Libby's supposed to be at home with her family enjoying life, not locked up in the foster system." Peter paced. "She's too sweet and good." He turned to his mom, tears rolling down his face. "She has no one, Mom, no one." His words fell to a whisper. "I'm it. I was all she had and now she thinks I abandoned her, too!"

He paced like a caged animal, his jaw set. He stopped at the side of the monstrous speakers and pounded them with both fists. A mournful groan roared from him, startling the many who watched. He braced his head on the speakers, trying to keep control. His arms shook with rage.

All he could feel was the cutting pain of a broken heart. His love for a sweet, helpless girl tore at him.

He turned and grabbed the edge of a heavy equipment table and upended it like a toy. Expensive equipment crashed to the ground. The onlookers exchanged concerned glances. Peter didn't care. He had never behaved like this. He was the quiet one, the bandleader they all counted on no matter what.

His father walked out from backstage where he observed the exchange. "That's enough, Peter, take a walk." He spoke quietly, but with a steel tone. "We have a sold-out show tonight. Pull yourself together."

Peter glared at his father, in tortured agony. "You did this." Venom tinged his voice.

Without a word or a glance to anyone, Peter walked off the stage and out of the arena.

He pulled his hood up to disappear from the world, and thrust his hands deep into his pockets as he braced against the cold December air. Not even the collection of fans gathered to catch an early peek at the Jamieson brothers noticed the brooding young man walk from the arena.

His emotions strung tight; he didn't know what to do. *Damn it!* Everything about this situation was wrong. So he wandered the streets, not stopping, not pausing, losing track of the world around him. He didn't care about the band, the preconcert interviews, or the demanding fans. In any other situation, he would put all these things before personal stuff, but not today. Libby had needed him and he was supposed to be there for her. He had all the money and the power. He needed to pull her out of the terrible life forced upon her. But there was no place to go. Who would help him? How could he ever find her?

He walked on. Hollow. Empty.

His throat choked up like a vise. He trudged on as the late afternoon sun set, and winter darkness threw a cold, heavy blanket over his world.

Was she okay? A foster home sounded scary and dangerous. He'd heard about kids being mistreated in foster homes. Libby was his rock, but she was also a fragile soul. She'd lost too much.

The wind picked up and tiny shards of sleet whipped

at him as he pushed forward. The sharp sting of ice hit his face. His emotions deadened, his whole being numb.

He walked on.

Much later, he shook off the haze and realized he didn't know the time or where he was. He'd walked so long, locked in his thoughts. It was dark; the stores were closed for the night. He peered in a nearby window. It was well after eight.

Shit. The warm-up band would be finished, and Jamieson was supposed to take the stage any minute. He stood on the cold, empty sidewalk and battled with himself. He wanted to walk forever and never go back, but an inner voice stopped him. *Damn it!* His sense of responsibility won. He turned back in the direction of the arena. He must be several miles away. He didn't have his phone but did have his wallet. He picked up the pace and started to jog. After a few blocks, he hailed a cab.

"Nokia Arena, please." He climbed into the warm vehicle. "How long will it take?"

"Fifteen minutes or more in this traffic. There's a big concert tonight," the cabbie replied.

"Yeah, I know." Peter reached back and pulled out his wallet. "Make it as quick as you can." He slipped several twenty-dollar bills through the payment slot. "Stage door, please."

He leaned his head back against the seat, staring blankly. His body began to shiver, but not from the cold.

Ten minutes later, Peter stepped out of the cab, passed the security detail at the stage door, and ran backstage. The crammed area held dozens more people than normal, everyone in a panic.

All eyes turned to Peter.

"Where the hell have you been?" his father bellowed. "Do you know what time it is? There are thousands of fans who paid a lot of money to see Jamieson tonight."

"I'm here now," Peter said through clenched teeth as he moved through the crowded space, ignoring all.

A loud chant of "Jamieson, Jamieson, Jamieson," echoed from the fans out front.

"Thank God. You had me scared to death." His mother rushed forward and hugged him tightly. "You're freezing. Oh, honey, where've you been?"

He shook off her embrace and walked past the crew and technicians as they yelled into radios and rushed around to start the show. He stepped onto the lift that would deliver him to his grand entrance, the muscles in his shoulders tight knots.

The music in the arena rose to epic levels as techies used hand signals to indicate the show was a go, and the countdown started. A fog machine filled the stage in a mysterious haze as lights and lasers glowed.

"Are you ready to party?!" The announcer's voice boomed over the mammoth speaker system. The crowd responded in a deafening roar.

"Jeez, Pete, could you screw up any more?" Garrett looked ready to blow.

Peter stared through him, unconcerned. He wanted this night over.

"You wearing that?" Adam asked, guitar in hand.

Peter looked down at the sleet-soaked sweatshirt, pulled it over his head, and flung it away, revealing a ragged T-shirt. He stared straight ahead, seeing nothing, his chest tight and suffocating.

Adam and Garrett exchanged concerned looks; Peter ignored them. A tech ran up and attached his headset, securing it quickly without a word. Around them, chaos reigned as the crew launched the show. The lift jerked and rose as spotlights circled the stage and the announcer spoke.

"Ladies and gentlemen, Jamieson is in the building!"

The crowd erupted in screams. The lift stopped high above the stage. The view was staggering. The spots illuminated the three young entertainers, as if they were statues from the heavens.

This was the last place Peter wanted to be.

He stood lost in thought. It didn't even occur to him to start the show.

Garrett took over and gave the count. He and Adam hit the strings of their instruments, and the music of Jamieson filled the air. On autopilot, Peter went through all the motions of the concert. He channeled his anger and frustration into the pulsing music. His performance was intense, the light side of him nowhere to be seen. He sang each song with anger and pain. The tender ballads became mournful wails of emotion, the high-powered rock numbers a snarl of passion. His eyes closed as he lived each word.

It wasn't their normal upbeat, chatty concert, but there existed an incredible energy that no audience had ever witnessed. Peter felt drained with nothing left to give. The final encore ended, and the trio ran offstage.

"Way to channel that anger, Pete." Garrett smacked him on the back. "We need to piss you off more often."

"Screw you," Peter spat with a venomous glare. He ripped the headset off and whipped it across the room, then stormed out the same door he came in.

19

Peter was running out of ideas. He'd spent the last weeks since he learned Libby had been placed in a foster home trying to track her down, which wasn't easy when he was stuck in Europe on tour. He waited as his call was transferred. Praying the woman answered.

"Hello, this is Julie Orman."

Thank God. "Hi, Miss Orman, I was hoping you could help me. I'm trying to find a girl who recently went to your school. Her name is Libby Sawyer."

"Excuse me, who's calling?" she asked.

"I'm a friend of Libby's. She and I had a misunderstanding, and then I heard she left town. I've been trying everything I can think of to track her down, but no one will help me."

"I'm sorry, the school isn't allowed to give out student information, particularly in a situation like hers," the woman explained politely yet firmly.

"Please, you have to help me. I've talked to people in Milwaukee, at the Department of Family Services, Child Welfare, and the foster system. No one will tell me anything. I didn't know where else to call." He was distraught and had exhausted all his options.

"I'd like to help you, I truly would. Libby was a special student to me, but you seem to already know as much as I do. I have also been trying to locate her and reach out to help. So far, the only people they'll release information to are her parents or guardians."

He exhaled, defeated.

"You aren't family, are you?" she asked.

"No," his answered. "I'm her boyfriend."

"Boyfriend? What is your name?" Miss Orman asked, sounding cautious.

"Peter Jamieson."

"Oh God."

"Excuse me?"

"Libby told me about you, but I wasn't too sure. You wouldn't happen to be in . . ."

"In a band? Yeah." He laughed. "Is that a bad thing?"

"No, I'm so sorry." Miss Orman sounded surprised. "Libby told me about you a few times, but I wasn't sure. Her situation is . . . unusual. I was beginning to think she dreamt you up."

Now that she knew his connection to Libby, he felt

sure this woman could help him. "We aren't the most obvious couple. Listen, I really need to know if she's okay. Do you know where her dad is? Did they find him? Is she with him?"

"No, they haven't been able to locate him. I wish they had. I'm sure he'd be worried sick. Since you know she's been put in the system already, I'm not breaking any rules. But that's all I know. I'm sure she's doing fine. It's got to be better than where she was."

He hoped the counselor spoke the truth.

"I wish I could help, I really do. I've been trying to locate her, but there is so much red tape blocking the process. Her caseworker hasn't returned any of my calls or emails. At this point, I don't know when I'll learn anything, if ever."

His heart fell. A heavy silence weighed between them, his despair palpable.

"Listen, Libby and I had a bit of a connection. It's possible she might contact me. If she does, I can have her get ahold of you. Or if I hear any news, I can let you know."

"That would be awesome. Thank you. You don't know how great that is to hear." It was so amazing to speak to someone who actually knew Libby and cared about her.

"Well, it's a long shot. I may never hear from her."

"But you might, and it's the best news I've heard in weeks." He gave her his cell number and their manager's office number, too. "I'm in Europe on tour, so I might not get your call. But leave a message, and it'll catch up to me. Miss Orman, I can't thank you enough."

"No problem. I'm happy to do anything I can."

Peter heard the sound of a school bell in the background.

"I've got to go, but, Peter, thanks for calling and good luck on your tour."

"Thank you." His spirits improved. At least one other person out there wanted to help Libby.

• • •

A few days later as the sound check dragged on, Peter sat on a stool mid-stage waiting as the engineers made adjustments. Each minute felt like an hour. He glanced up and noticed Adam and Garrett gesturing back and forth. When they noticed him watching, both froze.

"What?" Peter asked, irritated.

"Nothing," Garrett said.

"We have something to show you," Adam confessed. "But we don't want to upset you."

"What are you talking about?" he asked.

"You've been about to rip our heads off for the past week," Adam answered.

"Yeah, well. Sorry," Peter said, not meaning it. "Can we do it later?"

"No, we can't," Garrett stated, impatient. He spoke into

his mic: "Hey, Brian, play that video now, will ya?"

Peter saw concern in his brothers' eyes. Each held an acoustic guitar.

The lights in the arena dimmed. Garrett and Adam started to play.

An image of Libby, larger than life, filled the giant screens on each side of the stage. A smile lit her beautiful face; her blue eyes sparkled. Next came a picture of them talking, heads close as if sharing a secret. At first, Peter was confused, as he'd never seen the pictures before. He realized Adam's voyeuristic ways with his camera finally paid off. A few seconds later, another image appeared, this time of him and Libby sitting on the large boulder at Parfrey's Glen. Her long, blond hair blew in the breeze. Light freckles sprinkled her cheeks and a look of utter contentment shone on her face.

Transfixed, Peter moved across the stage for a direct view, never taking his eyes off the screen. Photo after photo appeared before him. Many showed the two of them together laughing, all with the beautiful backdrop of Parfrey's Glen. He had no idea Adam had taken all these pictures on that perfect September day. It seemed like a lifetime ago.

As the images continued to materialize across the screen, his brothers played an achingly familiar tune. The song he wrote for Libby: "Angel Kisses."

Peter released a breath that he felt he'd been holding

for days. This was their tribute to her, for him. Garrett and Adam never understood how much he cared about her until she was torn away.

When the song ended, a final photo filled the screen of the two of them walking up the path toward the bus. Her hand held firmly in his, she gazed up at him with total trust. Every emotion of love revealed on her face.

He missed her with every ounce of his soul, but now he had a bit of her back. Her image remained on the screen after the music ended.

Adam stepped next to him. "I thought you might like this. We could play your song with this video playing in the background."

Garrett stepped beside him and placed a firm hand on his shoulder. "I've been a jerk, and I was wrong. I didn't realize how much she meant to you. I guess I was jealous of how happy you were. I took her away from you and that was wrong. Here's a little bit of her back. It might give you a reason to want to sing again." Garrett's eyes searched Peter's. Peter saw the heartfelt remorse from his brother. He nodded his forgiveness.

"Yeah, I'd like that." His voice cracked. Maybe his brothers weren't so bad after all.

• • •

Libby tried to cry out for help but didn't get a chance. Sophie grabbed her by the hair and slammed her face against the wall. Then she grabbed Libby's arm and twisted it behind her back. Piercing pain shot up her arm and shoulder. Sophie shoved her against the sandy-textured paint, scraping her face raw.

"Listen, bitch, don't you ever cross me again. If you say one more word to Scott about me, I'll break your arm."

Libby didn't doubt it for a moment. Paralyzed with pain, she tried not to breathe. She prayed for Sophie to release her. The girl was crazy. She bit back her tears.

"And when I say something's mine, you just shut your whiny little trap and mind your own business."

Thankfully, Libby saw Scott, their twenty-three-year-old "adult in charge," walk around the corner, surprised. He rushed over.

"Sophie, what are you doing? Let go of her."

"Just having a little chat here. Libby had a crick in her back and I'm trying to straighten her out." Her viselike grip tightened.

"Let her go. Right now!" His raised voice brought Michael and BJ from the kitchen.

"Shit, Sophie, what did she do to piss you off?" Michael chewed on a Pop-Tart as he spoke.

BJ looked on, a satisfied smirk on his big, dumb face.

"Feeling better now?" Sophie asked, getting up in Libby's face.

"Yeah." She groaned through clenched teeth. "Great."

"Sophie, I said now!" Scott yelled.

Sophie stuck her elbow in Libby's back before releasing her. "Anytime you need a little adjustment, let me know."

Libby leaned against the wall for support, unable to bear the pain of straightening her arm. Slowly, she relaxed enough for the limb to fall useless at her side. With her other hand, she pushed away from the wall, her cheek aching and bruised, the wall marred with a streak of blood.

"Sophie, you're killing me here. I thought you weren't going to allow your temper to get out of control," Scott said, this situation far beyond his limited skill set.

"Yeah, well, it sneaks out once in a while. I'm sorry. It'll never happen again," she said, clearly not meaning a word.

"You're right about that." Scott shook his head.

"Damn, Sophie! You're goin' back to juvie. It's three strikes and you're out," Michael happily taunted.

"I'm afraid he's right." Scott wrung his hands. "I've got to call this in."

"Yeah, well, screw you!" Sophie spat at Scott. "You're such an idiot."

"Sophie, go sit in the kitchen while I handle this. BJ, please stay with her while I talk to Libby."

Scott checked Libby for injuries and congratulated her for trying to get a peaceful resolution. Apparently, not fighting back or defending yourself qualified as good behavior. He told her to shower so she could clean off the sand and paint ground into her face. Today, he'd allow her to go in to school late. *Yippee.* She was sick and tired of being pushed around.

After her shower, she gave a report to the police about Sophie stealing her Jamieson CD. Narcing seemed like a lame reason to be pummeled against a wall, but the CD was the only thing she had left that tied her to Peter. She refused to put up with Sophie's constant bullying anymore.

In fact, she was done taking everybody's crap. She'd spent nearly two years doing what everyone else told her to. She'd been the model orphan child. No more! She'd been lied to, misled, and manipulated. There was no one left who cared about her; they'd all left or been taken away. Feeling sorry for herself wouldn't help, either. It was time to stop cowering in submission as other people made bad decisions for her.

Today this madness stopped. Libby refused to sit in this crappy house and get bullied and beat up. She'd been afraid for too long. That ended now. Today she would take back her life. Sink or swim, she'd do it on her own. She knew she could.

The decision made, Libby moved through her room with purpose. She dumped the schoolbooks and papers out of her backpack and kicked them under the bed. She went to the dresser and surveyed the contents. She grabbed a pair of jeans, three warm tops, a couple pairs of socks and underwear, an extra bra. Then she pulled a thick sweatshirt over the one she already wore. She dropped her makeup bag into the backpack, then pulled it back out. It took up too much space. She opened the bag, grabbed blush and mascara, dropped them into the pack and left the rest on the dresser.

She cushioned the picture of her family by wrapping it inside a T-shirt and then placed it in the middle of the pack. She moved around the room, scanning each item for something she might need in her future life. Nothing.

Her eyes settled on her narrow bed. Without pause, she went to the far side and reached deep between the mattress and box spring. She pulled out a bank envelope full of money she stashed from her job. She counted one hundred and fifty-three dollars, not nearly enough. She stuffed the cash in her back pocket. She opened the closet and examined the contents, a few shirts, several pairs of shoes, and the dress from homecoming that Miss Orman refused to take back. She left it all. She needed nothing from this place.

She looked at Sophie's part of the room. Clothes littered the floor and the bed was unmade. She hesitated only a moment, then moved to the dresser and worked her way through it, drawer by drawer.

Bingo!

Inside the second drawer lay her Jamieson CD in its cracked case; she tucked it in her bag. In the next drawer, she found an empty cigarette container, inside of which she discovered a thick wad of bills and a couple of joints.

She dumped the filthy drugs into the drawer and scanned the bills, a couple hundred dollars. She thought twice about taking the loot, but figured Sophie probably stole it to begin with or earned it selling drugs. It made sense that dirty money would help her now.

Satisfied, she checked the hall. She heard Scott on the phone in the kitchen. Libby stepped quietly to the front door, slipped into her coat, and grabbed Scott's warm gloves off the table. She needed these more than he did.

She exited the front door, pulling it quietly shut. She stood on the front porch and took a long deep breath. Libby Sawyer was finished, dead to her. She walked away from the house and never looked back.

My life begins today.

20

The spectacular view of Paris from the Eiffel Tower was wasted on Peter. He could only think about Libby and pray she was safe. As he gazed around the opulent room, he realized how far he and his brothers had come from their Texas childhood. But right now, he didn't care about any of it. He wandered the world-class restaurant, surrounded by affluent people, and checked his phone again.

One message.

He punched in his password, hoping this time to hear Libby on the other end. Each message became pure agony as he failed to find her cheery voice.

"Hi, Peter, this is Julie Orman from Rockville High School. Please call me as soon as you can."

He held his breath, hopeful. Perhaps this was the call he'd been waiting for, that she'd found Libby. Finally, he felt hope. He checked his watch, calculated the time difference, and dialed the number. He moved to the bank of windows on the side of the elegant room, away from the crowd. "Pick up, pick up," he said to himself as he gazed out at the stunning skyline.

"Hello, Julie Orman speaking."

"Hi, Miss Orman, this is Peter Jamieson, I just got your message. Did you find her?"

He heard her sigh. "Hi, Peter, I'm afraid I have some bad news. I wanted to get ahold of you right away."

"What is it?" His chest tightened as he braced himself.

"Child Welfare Services contacted me this afternoon. They placed Libby in a group home and not with a foster family as we thought." Her voice sounded sad.

"Oh no! Do you know where she is? Do you have a phone number?"

"No. I'm sorry. She ran away. Ten days ago. And there's been no sign of her since."

"Why would she do that? Are you sure?"

Miss Orman paused a moment and cleared her throat. "There was an altercation with another girl, and Libby got hurt."

Speechless, Peter raised his eyes to the stars outside.

"Is she hurt bad? Do they know where she went?" His voice became a whisper as he digested the news.

"I wish I had some answers for you. The authorities

are looking, but Libby's disappeared; she doesn't want to be found. If she contacts you, please let her know I'm here and want to help."

"I will." But she hadn't tried to call him since that first weekend she'd been gone. He didn't think she'd try again. She thought he dumped her. Peter's heart dropped. "Do you think they'll find her?" His mind began to reel. Too many possibilities. Too many unanswered questions.

"She's fallen off the radar. They've all but given up. She hasn't shown up in her old neighborhood in Michigan; there's no sign of her here in Rockville. I don't know what to do." Miss Orman's voice sounded heavy with emotion. "I pray she's okay. I'm so sorry. I feel I let her down."

Silence hung between them.

"I know, me too. Thank you for calling. I've got to hang up," he said before he broke down. He slid the phone closed. Around him the room buzzed with excitement. The sound became a static white noise in his ears. He saw, but heard nothing. Libby was gone. There was no way to find her. How had life gone from perfect to this nightmare he couldn't wake up from?

Garrett and Adam walked over.

"Pete, what's up?" Garrett said.

He looked up from his stupor. "Nothing."

The other two exchanged a worried glance. He knew they'd been growing more concerned about him.

"At least nothing you care about." Peter looked around the room filled with happy friends and colleagues. "I gotta get outta here." Despair filled his eyes as he searched for the closest exit.

Garrett nodded to Adam. "You better get Mom. It's gotta be about Libby."

Adam took off, darting through the crowd of VIP attendees who sipped their cocktails, oblivious to the crisis. Garrett went after Peter. "Pete, wait up!"

Peter stopped and turned around in the staging area of the restaurant kitchen. Around them, a busy staff of waiters and chefs looked up from their work, surprised to see the superstar guests of honor in their kitchen.

"Is everything okay?" He searched Peter's face.

Peter offered nothing.

"Come on, dude, what's going on? What was that phone call about? Is it Libby?"

"Yeah, it was about Libby." Peter stood with his hands deep in his pockets, his voice heavy with emotion.

Their mother entered the kitchen and rushed over. "What happened?"

"She's gone," he whispered.

"Peter, everything is going to be okay." His mother tried to soothe him.

"No, it's not okay. It's never going to be okay. Don't you get it? She's gone. She ran away. No one can find her.

Libby's hiding and the authorities don't care. She's already become a statistic." Garrett, Adam, and his mother looked at one another, unsure what to say or do.

"She's out there alone, and she has nothing!" he screamed, fisting his hands in the air, silencing everyone. "I was all she had. Just me. I was it." He spoke to no one in particular, his body tense, a sheen of perspiration on his brow. "Everyone in her life has let her down, and now you can add my name to this list."

"They'll find her, Pete. Just give it time," Garrett said.

"Don't be an idiot; it's been ten days. Everyone she's ever trusted has let her down. She's gone!" The restaurant staff watched his uncomfortable tirade.

Peter slumped forward; his hands gripped the metal counter meant for food service. "Mom, I promised her. I promised I'd get her out of there. We had a plan. I was going to save her."

"I'm so sorry. We should have done something to help her. I just didn't realize how difficult her situation is."

"Of course it's difficult. Her life was ripped out from under her. She used to be just like us. She lived in suburbia with a happy family, and a dog in the backyard. Then life happened to her and sucked everything away. Damn you. All of you!" He looked from one family member to the next. "All you did was judge her and get in our way."

He gazed down at his Armani suit and designer shoes.

"Look at us, standing around like royalty with more than we ever imagined while she is homeless and alone in the middle of January. She has nothing left. Nothing." He pounded on the food prep table. "Where can she go? How will she live?"

"She'll find her way. It'll work out. Give her credit," Adam said.

Peter shoved Adam against the wall, knocking stacks of metal pans to the floor, creating a deafening clatter. "Yeah, I'm sure most sixteen-year-old girls alone on the streets do really well."

He released Adam, his hands trembling. Shock showed on his little brother's face. "It isn't like she'll go back to Rockville. I sure wouldn't. I know her better than that. They screwed her over."

"Maybe she'll find you. Maybe she'll be at a show one day," his mother offered.

"Right, she'll just stand up in her seat and call my name to let me know she's there. Or maybe she'll just walk up to the bus and knock on the door. Explain to me how this is going to work." He faced his mother; sadness filled his eyes.

Suddenly, cheers sounded from the next room. Their manager popped in. "You got it! You got nominated for album of the year! Can you believe it? We're going back to the Grammys! Get in here!"

They looked at one another, the contrast of their lives and Libby's painfully obvious.

• • •

Libby walked alone, her muscles sore from sitting on a bus too many hours. She liked the bus, though. Once on board, she disappeared in the back unseen. By the time she got off, several states later, a new driver sat up front.

This town was "middle of nowhere Georgia," as Peter would say. More than anything, she longed to talk to him, but knew those days were long gone.

As she wandered the streets of the small town of Pebble Creek, she wished for an easy solution to her problems. But it was far too late for easy. Her mother used to say, "Life can be an uphill battle, so you better keep your head down and keep climbing."

Who knew how true those words would prove to be? She thought about her mom a lot on the bus and the drastic changes in her life the past two years. It started as a happy, normal family, then fell into tragedy—a broken family and delinquent runaway. She realized she'd finally accepted her mother's and sister's death. The months of debilitating grief were past. Now the loss had become a part of who she was, but it no longer defined her. In fact, she believed they watched her from the heavens with love.

Her stomach grumbled and interrupted her thoughts.

With money running low, she needed to settle for a bit and this town seemed as good as any. She scanned each storefront in hopes of finding a help wanted sign. At this point, she'd be willing to do just about anything to make some money. Anything but go back to Rockville or the group home.

By the time she reached the edge of town, disappointment weighed on her shoulders like a heavy cloak. The last building before the road turned into the countryside was a battered motel called the Twilight. A vacancy sign blinked on and off, except for the broken last three letters. Scraggly weeds beat down the grass in sporadic patches around the perimeter. The motel could lead the list of tacky places to stay, but a real bed and a shower tempted her enough to approach.

The screen door squeaked as she entered a rundown office. A television blared cartoons from a backroom.

Libby stood in the middle of the small lobby, afraid to be noticed, but desperate to know if she could afford one night. A woman's voice yelled in the background. "Damien, stop poking your brother." The woman walked past the open doorway, looking up in time to see Libby.

"Hang on, hon, I'll be right with ya." Her voice sounded harried.

The young woman returned with a baby on her hip, her hair in a messy ponytail, and bags under her eyes.

"Can I help you?" she asked, eyeing Libby. "Well?"

"I'm sorry, I was just wondering, how much for a room?"

"Single or double?"

"Um, just a single."

"Forty-five bucks. Cash or credit card, no checks."

Libby mentally recounted her money. The toddler started to smell.

"I ain't got all day. Do you want it or not?"

"Yeah, I do." She stepped up to the scratched counter and dug in her pocket for cash.

"Sign in here." The woman pushed a small card at her, requesting her name and address.

Libby stared at the card, then, trying not to look nervous, grabbed the pen and signed the name Jill Munroe. It was the first name that popped into her head. Her mother always loved the television show *Charlie's Angels*. Jill Munroe was her favorite character, a beautiful, confident cop. Why she thought of that now, she couldn't guess. Libby made up an address, scribbled the signature, and pushed the card back toward the woman.

"That's forty-nine eighty-two with tax." She shifted the child to her other hip and peeked into the backroom. "Damien, get down from that cupboard right now or I'll tan your little hide. No more cookies!"

Libby counted out fifty dollars and placed it carefully on top of the card.

"That child will be the death of me yet, the rotten little bugger. Just like his father."

Libby smiled weakly and hoped the woman would remain distracted and not question why a teenager was renting a room at two o'clock on a Wednesday afternoon.

"Here you go, room six." She handed her the key and her change. "I've gotta get this one changed before I have a bigger mess on my hands." The woman scooped the cash and card behind the counter, then vanished into the chaos of the back room.

Libby picked up the key and then paused to be sure the clerk wouldn't return. When the coast was clear, she took a huge handful of candies from a dish on the counter. She walked with a skip in her step as she went to find her room. A clean bed, a warm shower—life was looking up.

The room turned out to be little more than a closet. The walls were thin and the fuzzy old television barely worked. The shower walls were marred by rusty water stains, but the faucet provided hot water. Between the tiny soap for shampoo and the touch of water, butter soft as it rolled over her, Libby hadn't felt this good in weeks. She spent more time under the spray washing out her panties and socks. Finally, exhaustion and wrinkled fingertips coaxed her to turn off the shower. After drying with a thin towel and hanging her undergarments over the shower rod, she fell into bed. Despite it being only late afternoon, she was asleep almost as soon as her head hit the pillow.

· · ·

Libby woke slowly. She'd slept straight through the evening to the next day. She sat up in bed and noticed her groggy reflection in the dresser's chipped mirror. Her hair was a mess of blond split ends; she couldn't remember the last time she'd trimmed it. The tangled strands fell to her waist. Dark circles shadowed below her eyes. She really needed mascara. Her adrenaline had been churning for so long from her fear of being caught that she'd let her looks go.

She needed to regroup and figure out what to do next. Her money would only pay for another night or two, and then she'd be out on her own again. While in Chicago, waiting overnight for the next bus south, she'd slept on the streets and spent most of the night terrified, freezing, and heartbroken.

She pushed the thoughts away. A pity party wouldn't solve anything. She got up and slipped into her dirty jeans and pulled on a cami and a long-sleeved shirt. Her socks were still damp, so she set them on the heat register and slipped into her tennis shoes. She pushed her cash deep into the front pocket of her jeans. Her life savings. It was meager, but enough to survive on for a couple more days.

After sliding the room key in her back pocket, she grabbed her coat and braved the cool January air.

The squeaky door of the office announced her arrival. The familiar drone of a kids' show seeped in from the next room. The frazzled voice of the desk clerk sounded as she popped her head around the doorway to see who interrupted. She held a phone to her ear. "Just a minute," she said, and disappeared behind the wall.

Libby examined the tourist pamphlets displayed in a rack while she waited for the conversation to end.

"No, I don't know when I'll be able to bring the kids again. I'm trying to keep this place afloat by myself, and Jimmy Junior's asthma is flaring up again. Jimmy, I'm not blaming you. I'm doing the best I can is all. I gotta go, I've got a customer."

Libby heard the phone clunk back onto the cradle and pretended to read a brochure about underground caves.

"Men," the woman said, coming back around the corner. "You certainly can't live with 'em and it's near impossible to live without 'em." She pushed her bleached hair out of her flushed face. "You checking out?"

"Uh, no. Do I have to yet?" Libby didn't realize she'd have to check out so soon.

"No, checkout's at eleven, but I can give you till twelve if you need it, not like I'm gonna get to cleaning your room anytime soon."

"Actually, I was thinking of one more night."

"Whatever suits you. Anything else?" She clicked her polished fingertips on the counter.

"Yes, I was wondering if you have a scissors I could borrow."

"Let's see. There should be one around here somewhere." She rifled through drawers and shuffled papers. "Whatcha need it for?"

Libby's face warmed. She wanted to lie, but couldn't think fast enough. "For my hair."

The woman examined Libby closely. "I see. Needing a new look, are you?"

Libby nodded.

"Well, who am I to interfere? It's your business. Here you go." She handed over a pair of scissors. "Be sure to return them."

"I will, I promise." Libby took them and quickly went to her room.

Less than thirty minutes later, Libby returned the scissors. The woman stood behind the counter, adding numbers on a small desk calculator. She looked up as Libby entered.

"Well, let's see your handiwork."

Libby turned around, revealing her shortened tresses. She'd meant for her hair to reach below her shoulders, but the length was crooked and each time she tried to fix it, the other side became uneven.

"Oh, honey, that's the worst haircut I've ever seen."

Libby's heart fell. She knew it wasn't great, but she didn't realize it was that bad.

"Come around back here, and I'll fix it up if you like."

Libby hesitated, not sure if she should.

"Come on, I won't bite your head off. I'm pretty handy with a scissors. I cut all my boys' hair, saves a heap a money. I cut Jimmy's hair, too, up until he got arrested and sent off to prison. That man is a fool if ever I saw one."

"Well, if you're sure."

"Course I am. I was all signed up for cosmetology school when I got pregnant with Jimmy Junior. Shattered my dreams until I saw the little bugger. Cutest thing you ever did see. By the way, I'm DarLynn."

"I'm Jill." She offered her hand along with the fake name. It would be a long time before she trusted someone with the truth.

"Nice to meet you, Jill." DarLynn shook her hand. "Take your coat off and sit right here." She pulled a small kitchen stool into the middle of her narrow kitchen.

Libby took off her coat, laid it on a sofa covered with an old bedspread, then sat on the stool. DarLynn grabbed a comb and worked through Libby's hacked-up hair.

"You just can't cut your own hair. Bangs yes, but the rest, forget it. Never works." She began to snip away, and Libby started to relax with the constant chatter.

"Not too many young girls come to stay at the Twilight, at least not without a guy hanging on 'em."

Libby worried this would happen. She couldn't talk about herself, or she'd get shipped back.

"Reminds me of myself at your age. Trouble everywhere I turned. Those were some awful times. At least till I met Jimmy. My lord, he was a good-looking piece of man. Don't get me wrong, he's still damn fine, just life's been catching up with him. You gotta boyfriend?"

"No. Not anymore." Libby pretended it didn't matter.

"I see. Well, honey, you're better off without him. If he was too dim to see how wonderful you are, he was the wrong one." She snipped and combed, then suddenly paused. "He didn't hit you, did he?" DarLynn popped in front of Libby, her face etched with concern.

"Oh no, nothing like that. He just broke it off. Actually, he had his brother do it."

DarLynn looked outraged. "That's terrible." She resumed her trimming. "I tell ya, I had a guy break up with me. He walked out of a restaurant while I was in the ladies' room. Can you imagine? Stuck me with the bill, too. Honey, I tell you, men are pigs. No getting around it."

She couldn't ever imagine Peter leaving her stranded on a date, but then again, he didn't bother to break up with her himself, either.

"He leave you for another girl? That's what a lot of 'em do."

"I don't think so, but he plays in a band, so I guess there could be someone else." Another girl hadn't occurred to her until now. It made her stomach hurt. Whether it was from lack of food or thinking about Peter she couldn't say.

"A musician. Oh, honey, love a rocker and your heart'll get broke every time. All those groupies pining away while they're up onstage playing, waiting for the end of the set so they can get their claws on him. You're definitely better off without him."

DarLynn examined her handiwork as if she were a high-priced stylist. "Not bad, if I say so myself. Gives you a fresh new look. That boy who dumped you wouldn't even know you now. Or anyone else who might be looking for you." She stood in front of Libby and held her eyes in knowing question. "Honey, you want me to call someone for you?"

The seconds ticked by.

"No, I'm fine."

There was no one out there to call. Not one person, except maybe the police. Heck, they didn't really care, either.

The phone rang loudly, interrupting Libby's thoughts.

"Hang on just a sec, while I get that."

While DarLynn spoke on the phone, Libby grabbed a broom and swept the hair from the kitchen floor and dumped it in the trash. She put her stool back under the kitchen counter then peeked into the next room and discovered the little boy, Damien, glued to a television show with talking vegetables. How simple his life was.

DarLynn hung up. "You know, if it's not one thing, it's

another. That was school. Jimmy Junior's having another asthma attack. I've gotta pack up this crew and get him to the doctor. Again." She sighed, lifted the sleeping baby out of the swing, and laid him on the floor to stuff him into a coat. "When little Jimmy was born, I told his daddy not to smoke around him, but that man never listened to me a day of his life."

"Can I help?"

"No, I got it, but could you grab Damien's coat over there and get him into it?"

Libby reached for the miniature-sized coat.

"No, Momma, I don't wanna go." Damien slipped away from Libby and dove onto the couch.

"I can stay with the kids. If you want," Libby offered.

"Really? Are you sure?" DarLynn hesitated. "Does it make me a bad mother to leave them with a stranger? Hauling this mangy bunch takes every bit of energy I've got, plus when I get back I've got rooms to clean."

"It's okay. I've got nowhere to go, other than to look for a job. I really don't mind. You trimmed my hair, so this will help pay you back."

"Well, okay, there's a bottle in the fridge, and Damien likes mac and cheese. I've got plenty of food, so help yourself. You must be hungry, so don't be shy." She handed the sleeping baby to Libby. "I'll have my cell phone, so I'll call you if it gets too long. The number is taped to the fridge if you need anything." She pulled her coat on, grabbed an oversized purse, and threw it over her shoulder.

"Don't worry. I'll take care of everything." Libby looked down into the innocent little face of the baby. He felt warm and smelled of milk and fabric softener.

"Be good boys. Momma will be back soon." She kissed them both and dashed out the front door and into a rusty old pickup.

Libby sat on the couch, the baby cradled close, with Damien on her other side. Holding the innocent babe filled a void. For once she felt a purpose, a meaning in this world. It might be a small thing, but helping DarLynn was the most important thing she'd done in a long time.

Two hours later, Libby had fed the boys, stuffed herself with food, and tidied the small living area. DarLynn returned with a tow-headed boy about five or six years old and a prescription bag.

"I see the place is still standing. I can't thank you enough." She looked around at the clean counters and organized room. "Oh my gosh, you did the dishes. You didn't need to do that, but honey, I've been trying to get to them since yesterday morning, never enough hours in a day. Thank you. I hope you got a bite to eat."

"Yes, thank you, I did." Libby smiled.

"You're a lifesaver. How can I thank you?"

"You don't need to thank me. You trimmed my hair, and trust me, I ate a lot."

"Well, it's my pleasure, but how 'bout your room is on me tonight?"

Libby wanted to refuse and say she could pay her own way, but a free room would save her almost fifty dollars. "Are you sure?"

"Absolutely. We girls have got to stick together." She gave a knowing wink.

Libby warmed at her generosity. "Thank you."

"I don't know how long you were thinking of hanging around, but Penny needs a waitress down at the Fork in the Road. It's a café, nothing fancy, just a bunch of farmers and truckers coming through, but they're good people."

"Thanks, I think I'll check it out."

21

Six months later

"*Good* morning, Jerrold." Libby poured coffee for the kind older gentleman who had become her closest confidant, even closer than DarLynn.

"Morning, Jill." Jerrold knew her true identity, unlike the rest of the town. He kept his knowledge private under client-lawyer privilege, calling her by the name printed on the plastic name badge pinned to her waitress uniform.

Shortly after she started at the Fork in the Road, Jerrold became one of her regulars. Five mornings a week he came in for coffee, eggs basted, wheat toast, and a half grapefruit. They immediately hit it off. Jerrold retired two years before. His wife still worked the morning shift at the local hospital. Used to getting up early to work for the past forty-five years, he came in for breakfast each day. He always sat in Libby's section.

"Catch any fish yesterday?" Libby knew Jerrold struggled with retirement. He tried hard to keep his days full, fishing and puttering around his workshop, but his heart remained with his law practice. He spent his career working as a lawyer for Family Services.

When she first learned of his legal background, Libby feared he could see through her façade and would send her back to Wisconsin. Instead, he became her angel of mercy, guiding her through the mess of surviving as a teenage runaway.

"Yeah, I caught a couple, but threw them back." He drummed his fingers on the counter as if impatient. "I spent all evening reading." His head tilted to the side and a smirk lit his face.

Libby placed the coffeepot on the heating element behind her, then returned to Jerrold. "Anything good? All I ever get to read are textbooks."

"Oh, it's very good. It's a little something that arrived in the mail from the State of Georgia yesterday." He patted his pocket, where a white envelope stuck out. He grinned.

"Is that my letter?" He had her full attention. "Don't you dare tease me. Did my appeal pass?" She reached to snatch the envelope, but Jerrold blocked her move. "I'm not afraid to jump over this counter and take it from you." She twisted the towel that hung from her apron in impatience.

Jerrold took a slow sip of coffee. His eyes darted to everything in the diner except Libby. She slapped her hands on the counter in front of him.

"Listen here, old man. Give it up. Am I free? You can't withhold information from me. I'm your client." Jitters fluttered through her stomach. Her future depended on that envelope.

In what seemed like slow motion, he removed the envelope from his pocket, methodically pulled out the papers, then patted his pockets. "Where did I put my reading glasses?" His stalling tormented her.

"They're on your head," Libby pointed out in short, impatient words.

"Ah yes, so they are." He pulled the cheaters off his head, put them on, and began to scan the document line by line. "Hmm. Mmhmm. Yup, looks good."

"Oh for Pete's sake, get to the point." Libby wanted to strangle the man. "Give me the darn papers." She snatched them out of his hands and read. Her hands shook as she scanned the pages, looking for the magic words that would give her her freedom.

Then she saw it.

The petitioner, Elizabeth Ann Sawyer, has been granted a final decree of emancipation by the State of Georgia.

It was over. She was no longer a runaway or a ward of the state. Jerrold had navigated the process of filing papers for emancipation of a minor. Now she could make her own decisions, and no longer need a parent or guardian to decide her future. No more Aunt Marge, no more fear of group homes or anything else. Better than that, she could start college in the fall. For the last six months, Libby had worked her tail off getting her GED, taking the SAT, and applying to colleges. She'd been accepted to a school in Boston. For the first time in a long time, she felt her world glide into place.

She looked up at Jerrold. "It's done?"

"Yes." He nodded. "It's done."

"Woo-hoo!" She tossed the pages in the air.

Penny, owner of the Fork in the Road, peered around the corner. "Jill, what's all that racket about?"

Libby rushed to her side and hugged the plump woman and plastered a kiss on her cheek. "Penny, I just got the best news of my life."

"You win the lottery, hon?" Penny asked.

"Better than that. I'm free."

Penny's eyes moved to Jerrold, she nodded some unspoken words, and the two older people smiled. Apparently, Jerrold hadn't kept her situation entirely confidential after all.

• • •

After her shift ended, Libby returned to the motel with a box of cupcakes tucked under her arm. She all but floated down the street thinking of her newfound independence.

Now she was free to start college in the fall. She couldn't wait to get there. It was her lifelong dream. Between all the money she'd saved since landing in Pebble Creek, and the financial aid package Jerrold helped her apply for and get, no more obstacles stood in her way. She could do anything she wanted. Heck, she might even get her driver's license.

She entered the Twilight office and hollered out to the boys. Their sweet little heads popped around the counter. "Look what I've got." She opened the box to reveal five yummy cupcakes.

"Are those for us?"

Their lovable little faces warmed her heart. "Sure are. One for everybody." She smiled at her little buddies.

"Mom, too?" Jimmy Jr. asked.

"Absolutely. You want to pick one for her?" She held the box out while he carefully selected a pink cupcake with a flower on top. "Good choice." Libby ruffled his hair.

"Hey, Mom, look what Jill brought us." Damien ran around the front counter to the living quarters where DarLynn folded laundry. After one look at Libby, DarLynn bit her lip. She wore an odd expression.

"Is something wrong?" Libby set the box of cupcakes on the table.

DarLynn examined Libby as if she'd never seen her before. "Jill, where did you live before you came here?"

"Why do you ask?" She evaded the question, even

though she no longer needed to hide her past, thanks to Jerrold. Libby couldn't imagine why, after all these months, DarLynn would ask about her background. DarLynn had accepted Libby at face value, and they'd been great friends.

"You know how I like to watch all the entertainment shows." DarLynn pulled out a tiny hoodie from the laundry basket and attempted to straighten it. "Well, today there was a special interview with that big rock group, Jamieson."

Libby stopped in her tracks. She had tried not to think about Peter too much. It was difficult, because she'd often come across Jamieson in magazines DarLynn subscribed to. Peter was her secret love; she'd never forget him. Whenever she became scared or lonely, she allowed herself to linger over each moment they shared and savor their magical time. Sometimes she got carried away and daydreamed they were still together, planning their futures. But those thoughts wouldn't help her move on with life. Peter was best left in the recesses of her mind.

"Oh." She set the cupcakes on the table. She wanted to hear what DarLynn had to say, but also wanted to keep her memories of Peter private. Libby faced her friend, whose eyes scrutinized her.

"Yeah, it was really interesting. They have a new album out. They're doing a concert tour, but it's different than anything they've ever done before." DarLynn's voice sounded strained.

"That's nice, what are they doing?" Libby tried not to

care. Learning too much about Peter's life would only make her heartsick for him all over again. She worked hard to push away all the loss in her life and move forward.

"They're looking for a girl." DarLynn twisted the tiny shirt.

A stab of pain hit Libby in the heart. "Oh, what for? Their next video?" She gazed out the window and hated the idea of some strange girl in a video with Peter.

"No, actually, it's a girl one of the brothers used to date."

Libby's head snapped up. DarLynn's eyes blazed. Libby's mouth went dry. She didn't know what to say, so she returned her attention to staring out the window.

"In fact, they showed a couple pictures of her." DarLynn stepped closer.

Libby's gaze swung to the darkened television. Her heart felt heavy as she fought back emotions. Part of her worried about discovery, but then again, why would Peter want to find her? She was insignificant in the world of a rock band. This must be a promo to sell more CDs. It hurt to even hope.

"I recorded it and just got a chance to watch it." DarLynn picked up the remote and clicked on the television.

A couple more clicks, and DarLynn brought up the program. Peter appeared frozen on the screen, where DarLynn had paused the show. She hit PLAY, and Peter's voice filled the room. The sight of him tugged at Libby's heart. He still wore the pendant she gave him. She'd forgotten how handsome he looked. He explained that he and his brothers dedicated this tour to finding a girl he fell in love with and lost.

She moved toward the television, unaware of everything around her. She knelt before the screen and watched Peter explain his futile efforts to find this girl. A photo of Libby and Peter sitting on the giant rock at Parfrey's Glen flashed on the screen. She caught her breath. She remembered the moment clearly. It took place when Peter almost kissed her, but Adam interrupted. She smiled at the memory, reached up, and touched the screen with her fingertips.

DarLynn paused the image of Libby and Peter, their dreamy expressions focused on each other. Libby remembered every essence of Peter: the way his hair lay heavy across his brow, the deep color of his eyes, and the tilt of his mouth. Lost in thought, a few moments passed before DarLynn's words brought her back to reality.

"He says the girl's name is Libby." Kindness shone in DarLynn's eyes. "That girl in the picture is you."

The veil of secrecy lifted. Libby nodded to DarLynn as tears welled in her eyes.

22

The next day, Libby and DarLynn crowded in front of the computer at the Pebble Creek Public Library. There were only a few minutes left before they had to surrender the computer to the next user. Jamieson had created an internet survey to help screen fans and find Libby. Displayed on the screen were ten questions.

"What if I don't know the answers? I'll never get the free passes to the concert and I'll never get to see him." Now that Libby knew Peter wanted to find her, winning these tickets became her sole mission. She missed out on the earlier concerts, because she didn't know he was searching for her. The deadline for the Chicago concert ended last night. The only concert left was in Red Rocks, Colorado, more than a thousand miles away. She didn't know how they'd get there, but one step at a time.

"Of course you'll know the answers. He wrote the

survey for you." DarLynn grabbed the mouse and scrolled to the multiple-choice questions listed below. "Okay, Jill, I mean, Libby." DarLynn tilted her head to the side and aimed an annoyed yet friendly look at Libby. It was clear that DarLynn wasn't quite ready to let Libby off the hook for lying about her identity these past months.

Libby shrugged. What else could she do? At the time, she needed to be someone else.

"First question. Where did Peter and Libby meet?" DarLynn read.

Libby almost blurted out the answer when DarLynn shushed her. "No, no, let me see if I can get it right. '(A) a concert, (B) a restaurant, (C) a special appearance, (D) a nature preserve, (E) on their tour bus, (F) a theme park.'" DarLynn squinted at the screen as she mulled over the choices. "This is trickier than I thought. I'll say a theme park. That makes sense. Plus, a concert is too obvious." She moved to click on the theme park box.

"*Errt.*" Libby gave her best imitation of a game show buzzer. "Wrong. It's (D) nature preserve."

DarLynn shifted the mouse and clicked on NATURE PRESERVE. "Interesting. I'd have never guessed. Next question. 'What was Libby doing when they met? (A) talking, (B) eating, (C) drawing, (D) texting, (E) singing, (F) sleeping.' That one's easy, (C) drawing."

"*Ding, ding, ding.*" Libby grinned. Even when buried in work, Libby always kept a drawing pad, her lifeline, nearby.

DarLynn read through the next couple questions and guessed wrong each time. It gave Libby hope that all the random girls out there who wanted to meet Peter would guess wrong as well. She moved to the next question.

"'What is Libby's sister's name?'" DarLynn looked back at Libby, sadness in her eyes. "I'm sorry, Jill. I still can't believe you lost both your momma and your sister." She reached out and gave Libby a quick hug.

Libby didn't correct DarLynn for using the wrong name again. She took the mouse and clicked on the name SARAH. "Keep going, read the next one." Libby didn't want to think about Sarah right now, and what a powerful question Peter left for her. No one could possibly know the answer unless they knew Libby back in Michigan. Everyone else would have to guess.

"Last question," DarLynn read. "'Where was Libby when Peter's dad suffered a heart attack?'" DarLynn turned to her. "Holy moly, girl, you've led a busy life."

Libby aimed a crooked smile at her. DarLynn didn't know the half of it.

"Let's see, '(A) at school, (B) at home, (C) at a football game, (D) at a dance, (E) at work, or (F) with Peter.' Hmm." DarLynn focused on the computer and studied each answer as if it were a college entrance exam. She glanced at Libby, hoping for a hint. "With Peter. You were with Peter when his father had a heart attack."

"*Errt.* Wrong again. The answer is (D) at a dance."

DarLynn shook her head as she clicked the D box.

Music suddenly blared from the computer speakers, and the screen changed to a banner that read, CONGRATULATIONS! YOU'VE ANSWERED ALL QUESTIONS CORRECTLY. TO REDEEM YOUR TWO FREE PASSES FOR JAMIESON'S RED ROCKS, COLORADO, CONCERT, ENTER YOUR EMAIL ADDRESS.

"I don't have an email address." Libby panicked that she was so close and yet another hurdle blocked her from Peter.

"Don't worry, we can open one for you. It only takes a couple minutes." DarLynn clicked open another screen.

"Excuse me," the librarian interrupted. "Your time has expired and you need to vacate this computer for the next person."

"We just need a few more minutes. Please," Libby pleaded.

"I'm sorry. It will set back the whole schedule and we're already running over. If I give you extra time, then so will the next person and the next. Your time is up, but you can sign up for another session later."

If the woman weren't so nice about it, Libby would have been mad.

"DarLynn, what do we do?"

"Don't get yer undies in a bundle." She punched in a couple more keys and hit ENTER. "Got it!"

A message appeared on the screen instructing them to print the pass for the concert from their email account. DarLynn hit PRINT.

"Thank you!" Libby hugged her tightly.

Libby and DarLynn eagerly watched the paper appear from the printer, paid their ten-cent copy fee, and rushed out of the library. "How did you set up an email account so fast?"

"I didn't. I knew we only had a few seconds, so I entered in my info. I used your name, just my email. It's all good."

• • •

"Hey, Pete, we got another one." Garrett yelled across the presidential suite of the Intercontinental Hotel.

Peter braced himself and tried not to get his hopes up. Garrett took it upon himself to monitor the incoming "Libby" surveys. He still felt guilty for all the damage he'd done. Keeping track of the surveys was not an easy job, Peter knew, since the site received thousands of hits a day. Fortunately, the survey system only forwarded entries with all the questions answered correctly.

"Yeah?" Peter crossed the plush carpet to the laptop. "I don't know. This seemed like such a good idea a couple of months ago, but all it's doing is turning our female fans into private eyes, code breakers, and little liars."

When he created this contest to find Libby, it was like the floodgates opened in cyberspace. Everyone wanted to win the prize—seats to a show and the chance to meet Peter Jamieson. A huge network of followers worked the odds and figured out the right answers. The odds of randomly getting all ten questions correct, with six possible answers each, were slim. However, as the search went on, more girls worked the odds and got them right.

"Why in the world should I think this one will be Libby?" His frustration at not finding her was beginning to get the best of him. She was out there somewhere and he couldn't find her.

Garrett grimaced. "I don't know. You have to believe. If you stop trying, you'll never find her. This could be her, and when she shows up at Red Rocks, answers the final question correctly, and gets backstage, it'll all be worth it."

He was right. Peter felt desperate to find Libby, and together the three brothers promoted the search contest everywhere. They did radio and television interviews, put it on Facebook, Twitter, and their blog. Garrett even made sure it hit all the fan magazines, but time was running out. Only one concert remained.

"Okay, where's she from?"

"Pebble Creek, Georgia." Garrett scrolled down the screen. "Aw, never mind. Her name isn't even Libby. That was dumb. Why would a girl pretend to be Libby and then use a different name?"

They'd revealed the fact that Libby was her first name, but didn't reveal her last name or any other details. "What name did she use?" Peter raised his water bottle for a drink.

"Jill Munroe."

Peter froze, the bottle inches from his mouth. "What

did you say?" He lowered the bottle and turned to the computer screen.

"Jill Munroe, why? Does that mean something?"

Peter stared at the name on the screen. "Yeah, it does. She told me once that her mom loved *Charlie's Angels* back in the seventies, and almost named her Jill after the character, Jill Munroe, but her dad refused." He grinned at Garrett and smacked him on the back. "You found her, man, that's her." Peter turned to leave the hotel suite.

"Where you going?" Garrett asked.

"Pebble Creek, Georgia. Where else?"

"Hold up, Romeo. You forgot something."

"What?" Peter scanned the room as he patted down his pockets to make sure he had his wallet and phone.

"A concert. Tonight. At Soldier Field."

"Aw, crap."

"You have about a hundred fans at the meet and greet. All those Libby wannabes." Garrett smirked, but Peter could see Garrett's relief that they'd found her.

The concert felt pointless now. He knew deep in his soul the girl, Jill Munroe from Pebble Creek, could only be Libby. There was no doubt in his mind. "Fine." He stood, hands on his hips, unsure what to do now that he had to wait until tomorrow.

"You might want to ask Roger to get you a flight out of here," Garrett prompted.

"Yeah, I'll do that."

"And you might want to call ahead."

"What for? I want to surprise her."

"Just in case, man. What if it isn't her?"

"It's her." With that, Peter left to find Roger, but couldn't resist a whoop and a punch of his fist in the air.

23

He decided to call ahead after all, but couldn't find a listing for Jill Munroe or Libby Sawyer.

He wanted to take the trip alone, but his mother wouldn't allow it. He'd made a lot of headway in winning more freedom from his family, but this time his mom wouldn't budge. "You are not traipsing across the country by yourself. Either take Roger, or wait to see her at Red Rocks."

So Roger it was. The next day, after flying into Atlanta, Peter and Roger drove to the tiny town of Pebble Creek. They drove down the quiet streets of the small town.

Libby was here, he felt it.

"Are you going to keep driving up and down the main drag or are we going to stop and ask someone?" Roger asked.

"I don't know. I thought this would be easier, and that I'd just bump into her."

"We could call the local radio station and tell them Peter Jamieson's here. That should bring her out, but I don't think this town even has a radio station. How about the police station? They ought to know everyone in town."

"No, Libby ran away. She doesn't need the police in her business." Peter pushed a hand through his hair and thought about how to find her. Knock door-to-door?

"In most small towns you go to the barbershop or the local diner if you want to know something," Roger said.

"I hardly think she's a regular at the barbershop. Let's try for a coffee shop." He drove slowly and searched for a restaurant. A couple blocks farther, where the road split, sat a quaint little restaurant, the Fork in the Road. He and Roger shared a grin. This felt right.

Peter pulled into a parking spot. "Do you mind waiting here? I'd like to do this myself."

"No problem, go ahead." Roger leaned back in his seat and closed his eyes, weary from their early morning flight.

Peter stepped out of the car and approached the front door of the restaurant. He combed his fingers through his hair to tidy it and smoothed down his T-shirt. A large wooden fork served as the handle for the front door. He took a deep breath, exhaled, and opened the door.

Inside, the café looked like a throwback to the sixties.

A long counter and stools faced the kitchen. Booths with faded red seats occupied each wall. Curtains decorated with tiny cherries covered the windows.

The place was busy for such a small town. A heavyset older woman bustled by, her arms loaded down with plates. "Grab a seat anywhere you want."

Peter wandered to the counter and sat on a stool. In front of him nested a napkin dispenser, ketchup and mustard bottles, and several menus in plastic sleeves. He gazed around the room, unsure where to begin. Should he start asking strangers if they knew Libby? Or Jill Munroe?

The waitress returned. "Do you know what you want, hon?" Her name tag read PENNY.

"Uh, no," he stuttered. "Actually, I wanted to ask you a question."

"I'll be right with you." Penny grabbed five plates from the kitchen counter and stacked them up her arm. With the other hand, she grabbed a coffeepot and disappeared.

Peter spun on his stool and watched her deliver the food to a family on the other side of the restaurant and then top off coffees. At the opposite end of the counter, he noticed an older gentleman reading a newspaper. Penny rushed past.

"Hold on one more sec," she said. "Jerrold, you ready for a refill?" The man with the newspaper held up his cup.

"You're running around like a chicken with her head cut off today," the man commented.

"Shorthanded for the next few days." Penny returned the pot to the burner and approached Peter. "All right, what'll you have?"

His hands began to sweat. Peter couldn't believe how nervous he was. Talking to strangers never rattled him, but the thought of seeing Libby again made him jumpy. "I'm looking for a friend of mine. I think she lives here, but I don't know where."

The woman tidied the counter as he spoke.

"Her name is Jill Munroe." He held his breath.

The woman stopped and looked at him. "You're looking for Jill?" Penny exchanged looks with the man at the end of the counter. He arched an eyebrow.

"Do you know her?" He tried to keep the desperation out of his voice.

"Sure, I know Jill." She hesitated. "But she's off today."

"Yes!" Peter slapped his hands on the counter. He struck gold. She worked here.

Penny watched him, wide-eyed. "How do you know Jill?"

"I met her in Wisconsin, almost a year ago. We used to date."

Penny nodded slowly and glanced again at the man with the newspaper.

"Can you tell me where she lives?" Peter looked from one to the other and back again. The man nodded at Penny.

"Sure thing. She lives at the Twilight motel on the west

edge of town. Works in the office most afternoons . . ."

"Thank you so much!" He popped off his stool and headed for the door. "I can't thank you enough." He waved at Penny as he left, ran to the car, and hopped in.

"Roger, she's here. I mean, not here like at the restaurant, but she works here. Except she's off today. She lives at the motel and works there, too." Peter started the car and sped off.

He drove west to the Twilight motel, a cheap roadside dive not fit for fleas. Roger gave him a cockeyed glance as Peter pulled into the gravel drive and parked in front of a blinking office sign. He couldn't imagine Libby actually lived here.

"You sure you want to do this?" Roger asked.

"Are you kidding me?" Peter left the rental car and entered the rundown office. The trill of a bell sounded as the door opened. Fortified with determination, Peter crossed the cracked linoleum to the front counter.

"Afternoon. Y'all looking for a room?" a middle-aged brassy blond asked. Her sickeningly sweet perfume overpowered him.

Peter almost took a step back when he saw her heavily painted face complete with crusty mascara and overdrawn lips coated in pink gloss.

"No, thank you. Actually, I'm looking for someone."

"Are you now? I've been looking for someone, too."

Peter nearly laughed. He might need Roger's help after

all. Heck, Roger might enjoy her. He offered his best man-
nered smile. "Actually, it's a friend of mine, who I believe
lives here. Her name is Jill."

"Oh." The desk clerk stood up. "She stays in number
six, since the phone doesn't work. Says she has no one to
call, but if I had a young man as sweet as you on my tail,
I'd sit by the phone all day waiting." She batted her oversized lashes; he wanted to run.

He eyed the door, his heart longing to be in room six,
but the flirty old woman prattled on.

"DarLynn, that's my daughter-in-law, lets Jill stay here.
She babysits the boys and watches the office while DarLynn's
at beauty school. She's gonna be a hairstylist. Don't know
why she needs to do that when she's got the Twilight to
run. This is my son Jimmy's place," she whispered as if it
were a big secret. "If it's good enough for him, it should be
good enough for her. Of course, Jimmy ain't happy about
her schoolin', but he's still got two more months to serve at
county—"

"Excuse me, ma'am," Peter interrupted for fear the
woman would never stop. "I think I'll go down to number
six and say hello."

"Of course. Look at me jabberin' away while you're
eager to see your friend. And she's a pretty one, too."

Peter moved toward the door. He couldn't wait to see
the look on Libby's face when she saw him.

"Oh, she ain't there," the woman called after him.

"She's not?" he nearly croaked in disbelief.

"Nope. She and DarLynn left in Jimmy's old Chevy early this morning; somethin' about a prize in Colorado. I think she won the lottery, but I don't know why she had to go way 'cross the country to turn in her ticket."

What was she talking about now? "Is she going to Red Rocks by chance?"

"That's right, now how'd you know that, with her not having a phone?"

"Just a good guess."

"Well, I've got a secret about her that I bet you'll never guess." She leaned forward.

"Her name isn't really Jill," she whispered, then paused for effect.

"No way?" Peter said, matching her quiet tone.

"It's Lynnie. She's been hiding out, but now with the lottery thing, she has to use her real name again."

He fought back a smile. "I never would have guessed that." He needed to prevent her from starting another long diatribe. At this rate, Roger would come looking for him. "Well, I should be heading out." He walked to the door.

"Wanna see her room?" the woman blurted.

Peter slowly turned back to her, a huge smile on his face. "I'd like that very much." If he couldn't see her in person at least he could see where she lived and make sure it was really her, even though his heart told him it was.

"By the way, my name's Beatrice, but my friends call me Bea." She snatched up a key and led him outside, standing a little too close for Peter's comfort.

He held his breath to avoid inhaling her odious perfume. He gave a pained look at Roger and waved him over. The large man hesitated but joined them.

"Bea, I'd like you to meet a very good friend of mine. This is Roger."

"Why, what a pleasure! Two good-lookin' men in one day. You must be the older brother." She held out her hand for Roger to kiss. He nearly choked, but shook her hand, which featured claw-length painted fingernails.

"Bea is going to show us Jill's room. Jill's not here right now. She's on her way to Colorado," Peter recited to Roger.

His friend nodded; understanding lit his eyes.

"She goin' to turn in her lottery ticket," Bea chimed in.

Roger turned a confused look on Peter.

"That's right." Peter grinned.

They followed Bea past a handful of rooms and paused at room six where she inserted the key. Bea turned to them. "You won't tattle on me, will you?" Her eyes focused on Roger. "I wouldn't want to get in trouble with DarLynn. She'd never let me watch the place again, and I love meeting new people."

"Not a word," Roger promised. "It'll be our little secret." He placed one hand on the door frame and leaned close to

Bea. Peter's pulse quickened as he pushed the door open and stepped into Libby's room.

So this is where she'd been. He walked through the small room. He ran his fingers over the faded bedspread. On the dresser sat a stack of books. Schoolbooks. Statistics, world history, psychology. Pride filled his heart. Libby stayed in school. He knew she was smart, but to live in this crummy motel, waitress, and still go to school, amazed him.

Roger blocked the doorway while Bea performed her best moves.

Peter turned and noticed a framed picture on the nightstand. His breath caught in his throat. He recognized a young, carefree Libby, her arms draped over a younger girl who could only be her little sister, Sarah. Her parents stood on each side of them. They were a beautiful family. The weight of all Libby had been through struck him full force. God, he wished she was here right now, but they'd be together again soon.

Reluctantly, he put the photo back in place.

Peter noticed Bea pressed up against Roger. "So then I went to Nashville to sing for this big record producer. He said he liked my style, said I had real panache, whatever that is." Bea fluttered her peacock lashes again.

He didn't have the heart to watch Roger suffer any longer. An assault from Bea had to be worse than Roger's tour of duty in Desert Storm.

"Roger," Peter interrupted. "I just realized we're going

to miss our flight if we don't head out." He efficiently pushed the two apart. "Bea, it's been a pleasure and I can't thank you enough for all your help."

He beelined to the car and started the engine. Roger literally leapt over the hood, slid in, and slammed his door. Bea flitted after Roger, her words still flying. Peter backed up, sped away, and pretended not to notice.

Roger glared at Peter. "You owe me big-time for that."

Peter howled in laughter and honked the horn as he cruised out of town, one step closer to Libby.

24

The next day, ominous clouds thundered over the Red Rocks Amphitheatre. "We are not canceling this concert," Peter said. "I don't care if there are torrential rains, earthquakes, or tsunamis; this show is happening." He glared at the Red Rocks stage manager, his posse of security, and the management team. Peter's family stood in formation behind him, a silent army of supporters.

"As I said before, it's not safe." The stage manager held his ground. "With an outdoor amphitheater, there are added dangers when inclement weather strikes."

"And I'll say it again, we are not canceling." Peter said, hands on his hips, a formidable opponent.

The stage manager looked to Peter's parents for help, but received none. "You don't understand. We have guidelines, policies, and insurance issues at stake here.

Do you want to take responsibility for that?"

"You bet I do. What do you need?" Peter didn't flinch. "Where do I sign? Do you want a check?" Too much rested on this concert. Libby was coming, and he would not let her be sent away.

"That's not how it works, and I'm sure your father can attest to that. We're talking about the safety of ten thousand people in and around the amphitheater."

His father interrupted. "Let's take a look at the radar once more." He gestured toward the computer screen nearby. "At this point, most of the fans are already in the stands or on the grounds. Canceling the concert isn't going to help. There must be some sort of emergency procedure when unexpected storms occur during a concert."

"Yes, of course there is. However, the goal is not to need them. Moving this many people can result in panic and injury. Plus, there is an added threat with a storm system of this magnitude."

"Don't you think it's a little late to send everyone home?" his mother said. "In fact, it would be irresponsible. According to the radar, this is a fast-moving system. Let's get the fans to safety here on the grounds, we will wait the storm out, and then all enjoy the concert. No one goes home disappointed."

"Well, I don't know. The stage will be soaked, and the seats in the stands will be wet. There will be no dry place to sit," the stage manager argued.

"The stage is simple. We can squeegee it off in minutes," Garrett said.

"Our fans never sit during a concert anyway," Adam added. "In fact, if you went out there and asked them if they want the concert canceled, or to take cover and come out when the storm passes, I guarantee they'll stay."

Peter watched the stage manager and his crew process the information and waffle. Libby was going to be here, and he'd be damned if a little rain would keep them apart.

"All right, but I want it on the record I don't like this decision."

"Thank you," his mom said. "We appreciate your flexibility to solve this problem. Let us know what we can do to help."

"You can have your crew cover the equipment and make sure everyone from your team is safely backstage when this storm hits."

• • •

Twenty minutes later, a few big fat raindrops pelted Peter. Seconds more, and the menacing clouds produced high winds. The crowd, as well as the band and crew, took cover. Red Rocks suffered a severe thunderstorm complete with spectacular lightning and quarter-sized hail. Peter hoped Libby was safe. He listened as the storm blazed through and left a trail of toppled souvenir tents and turned-over trash receptacles. But other than a lot of water and quick melting hail, no major damage occurred. The stage equipment stayed intact, and the fans eagerly came out from hiding.

While the Jamieson team prepped the stage, Peter's thoughts returned to finding Libby. "I know she's here," he said to Garrett. "She's had plenty of time to drive from Georgia." He watched the monitor setup backstage. It showed each girl who won contest tickets as she filled out the questionnaire. No Libby.

"So far, the security detail covering the contest area hasn't had anyone answer the final question correctly." Garrett looked worried.

"Where is she?" Peter said, staring at the security monitor.

• • •

"Come on, you miserable rust bucket, just one more mountain to climb." DarLynn gripped the steering wheel and concentrated on the gauges of the ancient pickup.

Libby chewed her lower lip as the engine groaned in protest. They were halfway up the steep entrance road to Red Rocks. Even though they left Georgia two days earlier, they arrived late. The truck caused problems the entire trip. First, an oil leak and then the engine overheated outside of Wichita.

She hoped the deluge of rain was a sign of cleansing

and would bring her good fortune and not an omen of bad luck. Libby could barely stay seated. She wanted to run the rest of the way.

A loud pop sounded from the engine and steam hissed out from under the hood, confirming her bad omen theory.

"Sweet baby Jesus, give us a break!" DarLynn pounded the steering wheel.

A parking attendant wearing an orange vest walked up. "Miss, you need to move your vehicle off the drive. You're blocking traffic."

"Does it look like I can move this beast? If you haven't noticed, we're having a little trouble here," DarLynn barked.

The man tried to hide his smirk. Apparently, he found their dying truck, spewing steam and oil, entertaining.

"Tell you what. If you can back your vehicle down to that service lot, you should be able to pull it in before it, ah, blows up." He grinned.

Despite her nerves over seeing Peter again, Libby smiled at the odds the truck would indeed explode.

"Stay with your vehicle, miss, and I'll get a tow truck on its way to help you out."

"But I have to get to the concert. I'm already late!" Libby peered out the window at him.

"That's right," DarLynn said. "She's Libby, the girl from the contest. They're looking for her."

"Right." The parking guy looked at them in doubt. "I heard something about a contest."

"Well, she's the one." DarLynn pointed at Libby. "We've driven halfway across the country to get her here, and we're not giving up. Libby, you hop out and run the rest of the way. I'll stay here and deal with the truck."

"Are you sure?" She wanted to go so badly, but hated to abandon DarLynn after everything she'd done for her.

"Don't you worry about me. I'll be waiting for you after the concert. Now go on."

Libby hugged her friend, then jumped out of the truck, ticket in hand. She showed it to the parking guy. "Do you know where Gate 3A is?"

His eyes widened as he recognized the VIP entrance. "All the way up. There are gold signs to direct you."

"Thank you." She smiled and ran around the bend in the road.

• • •

Out of breath after what seemed like a marathon trek, Libby arrived at the gate and joined the line under a gold banner that read SEARCH FOR LIBBY CONTEST WINNERS. Her nerves taut, she waited her turn.

"Ladies, patience please. We'll get you all back in. It's only a storm delay. Please show your ticket and hand stamp as you reenter," a tall, dark-haired security guy said.

Thankfully, the line moved quickly. Libby sighed in relief that the concert hadn't begun yet, but she felt annoyed at all the girls around her who pretended to be

"Peter's Libby." How could they have possibly answered all the contest questions right?

"Hand please," the security guard said.

"Excuse me?" Confused, Libby hesitated next to the turnstile with a black light set up.

"Your hand. Put it under the light so I can verify your hand stamp from exiting."

"I just got here."

"Oh." He grabbed the radio from his belt and spoke into it. "I've got a new arrival here; what do I do?" He turned back to Libby. "Sorry, since we had to evacuate the amphitheater there's been a lot of confusion. We're all manning different stations now."

The radio blared back. "Go to the contest table and have her complete the final question."

"This way," he said, stepping away from the main crush of fans reentering, and over to a long table with questionnaires, pens, and a surveillance camera set up in the corner. "Let's see, looks like you answer the question on this sheet and . . ." His radio blared again. "Hang on a sec." He took the radio and stepped away to listen.

Libby picked up the slip of paper and a pen. So this was how they would screen out all the girls pretending to be the real Libby? If all these girls could figure out the answers to the other questions, certainly they would know the answer to this one, too. She read the question.

"In the song 'Angel Kisses,' what is Peter referring to?"

She hugged the sheet to her and began to laugh. No one could possibly know the answer but her. She wrote the words on the paper. Her heart filled with joy at the memory of that autumn day when Peter traced her scarred hands with his fingertips and kissed her pain away.

She waited for the security guard, but he still spoke on his radio. Her adrenaline ran high now that she was about to see Peter again. Suddenly, music filled the air. The concert started, and she was missing it!

Anxious to find Peter, she waved to get the security man's attention. He held up his index finger and signaled he would be another minute. The crowd's roar filled her ears. She couldn't bear it. When he still didn't return, she waved again indicating that she left her answer sheet on the table. She turned and dashed away into the seating area to see Peter.

• • •

"Roger, you've got to speak up. I can't hear you over the music." The security guard held the radio tight to his ear and strained to hear what the head of Jamieson's security said.

"What is the status of the crowd at your entrance?" the voice crackled over the radio.

"We've got just about everyone back inside, but I still need to know about the contest procedure. I've got a girl who hasn't been processed yet, and no one else is here." He looked up to see the blond girl at the table wave to get his attention again. She pointed at the sheet on the table and then disappeared.

"Have her fill out the questionnaire and let me know her answer," Roger said.

"Got it." He spoke into the radio. "Hang on while I grab it and see what she wrote." He returned to the contest table, picked up her paper, and read the neatly printed words.

"'The scars on my hands.' That's what she wrote. Does it mean anything to you?" he asked.

"That's her! You found her! Bring her backstage!" Roger said.

"Dang it. I can't. She just entered the amphitheater. I'll never find her now."

25

Libby couldn't believe her eyes. Nestled between the massive red rocks lay an amazing amphitheater. Before her danced a sea of people. The stage lay at the bottom. Row after row of seats filled the hillside, all with a perfect view of Peter performing center stage. She nearly burst with excitement.

Several people brushed past as they returned to their seats. An usher approached and yelled something, but Libby couldn't hear a word over the pounding music. The woman shined a flashlight on the ticket in Libby's hand and gestured toward the audience. Did Libby know where her seat was?

"No," Libby yelled back, but knew her words were lost as the deafening sounds of Jamieson pumped through the speakers.

The woman read Libby's ticket and indicated she should follow. About fifteen rows from the stage, she illuminated the ticket for Libby and pointed out the seat number. Libby pressed her way into the row, but after she bumped and jostled past several people, she gave up and stayed where she was.

At this close distance she could feel the energy glowing off Peter. She screamed inside at the thrill of being so close and knowing he wanted to find her.

• • •

Peter couldn't see a damned thing. The intense spotlights limited his vision to about four feet past the stage. All he could do now is hope Roger would catch a glimpse of her on the monitor as she came through. He'd given up believing in the security personnel. They were more worried about kids sneaking in booze than finding a lone girl in the crowd.

They finished their first five songs. The energy in the amphitheater would have shot through the ceiling had there been one. Now that the storm had blown past, the sky shone crystal clear, and stars dotted the heavens. Peter signaled Adam to start the next number, then noticed his parents next to a waving Roger at stage right.

Peter ran to them, his heart pumping in anticipation, while Adam and Garrett vamped the opening of their next song. *Please let this be good news.* He looked hopefully at Roger, not daring to ask.

"She's here!" Roger shouted.

"Yes!" Peter shouted.

"But we don't know where," he continued. "Security didn't get her seat number and she disappeared into the audience."

"Yeah, but she's here!" He could dance on air.

Roger shook his head. He wasn't having nearly as much fun as Peter.

"So how do we find her? Any bright ideas?" Roger crossed his arms over his chest.

Garrett kept vamping onstage as Adam joked with the crowd. Peter could always count on Adam in a pinch. His dad looked frustrated that Peter was delaying the show.

"Yeah, actually I do. All the ticket winners had seats from row ten to row thirty. Get a couple of spotlights and start shining them on the crowd. See if you can spot her. If you don't find her in the next two songs, we'll send Adam and Garrett out while I do my solo. The crowd will never expect to see them roaming the aisles. They've both seen Libby up close and might find her."

Roger looked doubtful, but Peter spun away, ran across the stage, and slid into place between his brothers. Adam hit the chord and the next chart-topping song erupted from the speakers. Now that he knew Libby was in the house, he could barely contain himself. He gave it his all. He could see the spotlights roam over the crowd, but the stage lights made it impossible for him to see anyone clearly. He wasn't worried though. She was here and they'd find her.

. . .

Peter performed just like she remembered. His tall, lithe body moved with amazing power and grace. She'd almost forgotten his impossible good looks. Giant screens illuminated his every step. She nearly cried as she watched his familiar movements. How could she get to him? Maybe if she waited until after the concert?

The song ended and the lights softened. Garrett and Adam left the stage. A single light shone on Peter. He picked up a guitar and softly strummed. The audience cheered as they recognized the song.

He looked introspective as he spoke to the crowd.

"You may have heard that I've been trying to find a special someone from my past."

Her heart beat wildly. He was talking about her. She wanted to yell "I'm right here!" but the fans roared.

A huge smile covered his face. "Well, she's here tonight."

The masses thundered their approval.

"Libby, I know you're out there. I can feel it. Where are you?"

The sound of Peter speaking her name nearly brought

her to tears. She shouted, "I'm right here!" but the deafening cheers covered her words.

Peter laughed at the crowd's response, the sparkle in his eyes clear even from where she stood.

"I had a feeling that wasn't going to work." He continued to strum his guitar. "Tell you what, while I try to figure out how to find her in this huge audience, you enjoy this next song. It's called 'Angel Kisses,' and I wrote it for Libby."

As the horde of admirers delivered another deafening roar, Libby watched, transfixed. Her love for him skyrocketed as she watched. His beautiful baritone voice caressed each word. She remembered that day so long ago at Parfrey's Glen. Goose bumps covered her arms as he sang of a tender love that no one understood, and how "angel kisses" could wash away the scars of life.

Spotlights continued to wander over the crowd, but to Libby, she and Peter stood alone among the red rocks. The thousands of onlookers evaporated into the night.

• • •

Oblivious to her surroundings, Libby was surprised when halfway through the song someone tapped her on the arm. A young guy wearing a baseball hat and hoodie peered at her.

"Libby?"

He knew her name? She looked closer at his face. "Adam?!" She couldn't believe it. He'd changed so much.

He stood taller and looked older. He responded with his familiar adorable grin. Perhaps he hadn't changed much after all. He took her by the arm and pulled her toward the aisle, where he waved to a couple of techies. "Clear the way, boys."

"So, you're Libby?" one asked.

She nodded, embarrassed at the attention. The tech guys led a path through the fans who stood in the aisle. Adam took Libby by the arm and guided her as they approached the stage.

Suddenly, a wave of fear struck her. The moment was here. Her reunion with Peter was about to happen in front of this mass of fans. As they walked down the final steps, she glanced up and saw the image of her and Adam appear on the giant screens. A camera followed their progress toward the stage. The crowd caught on. She was the girl in the pictures. After all the promotion and news of Peter's "search for Libby," his fans knew she and Peter were about to be reunited and they would all enjoy front-row tickets. Before, her pulse simply raced; now it beat a staccato rhythm faster than a snare drum.

The tech guys pulled out a set of steps from under the stage and hoisted her up. She glanced back at Adam, scared.

"It's okay," he said, a relaxed, happy expression on his face.

She climbed the last stairs alone. Excited. And terrified. She stepped onto the stage. Peter stood at the other end, singing with his heart and soul.

Peter looked across the stage and saw her. He stopped singing and froze. Emotion clouded his eyes. He seemed to move in slow motion as he pushed his guitar so it hung behind his back. He walked toward her. The spectators erupted in cheers.

Libby's legs felt weak. She feared she might faint.

He searched her face as he came closer. Anguish filled his eyes. She could see all the pain and heartbreak they both had suffered. He rushed to her.

Her surroundings forgotten, she ran into his arms, oblivious to the roar of the audience, the lights, and the cameras. He pulled her into a tight embrace and swung her in the air. Finally. Her world felt whole again. He held her as if he would never let her go, and she wasn't sure she would let him. He moved with her and rocked her to the beat of the backup music. She remembered his strong, solid body and reveled in the joy of feeling it once again. Their eyes met and spoke of love and longing. The past hadn't changed. They were back in Wisconsin alone at Parfrey's Glen. Tears trailed down her cheeks. He held her face and kissed her in front of all those people and with the concert at a standstill. He kissed her for the long months they'd been apart and the promise of a future together.

26

Peter wouldn't let her out of his sight. She'd never felt so pampered in all her life. Everyone was so nice. Suddenly, she turned into a VIP on the Jamieson tour. The biggest surprise was Peter's mother. After being introduced, she welcomed Libby with open arms and hugged her close.

Security brought DarLynn backstage. The parking attendant eventually believed their story about Libby being "the girl," and he got DarLynn inside to see the concert. Together, they left Red Rocks in the Jamieson tour bus.

Libby had never seen anything so fancy in her life. Plush carpet covered the floors. The back of the bus featured a large-screen TV and comfy seating for a small crowd. Guitars were secured to the walls as décor and for easy access. The rolling reunion bus took them to an upscale hotel in downtown Denver. Jamieson occupied the entire executive floor. Peter's parents were super generous and gave a suite to Libby and DarLynn.

Libby and Peter talked late into the night. She dredged up all that happened to her from the drug bust, the horrors of the group home, and her eventual escape. Peter relived the experience with her as she recalled the painful memories. She shared stories about the kind people of Pebble Creek, how Jerrold helped her navigate the legal system, and her plans for college in the fall.

DarLynn stayed up late, keeping an eye on them from afar, but eventually climbed into her plush king bed. She left the door open to the sitting area to remind them of her presence.

Peter told Libby about their new album and that most of the songs were about her. He shared news that he planned to buy his own place. While he loved his family, he needed more independence and time away from their constant intrusion. He even convinced his parents to agree on a second tour bus so they all could enjoy more privacy. Late in the night, they finally fell asleep, snuggled together in a tangle of limbs on the sofa.

Morning arrived too early with the sound of DarLynn filling the whirlpool tub. Libby woke and snuggled into the comfort of Peter's arms, unwilling to leave his side. A loud knock and the sound of the suite door opening forced them upright.

"Good morning," Peter's mother sang brightly.

Peter groaned. "Mom, this is child abuse. I should have

you arrested for waking us up so early." He tossed a throw pillow at her.

"Doesn't look like you two got much sleep." She gave them a pointed look, bustled into the room, and returned the pillow to the sofa. "You kids don't need to use up all your words the first day."

"See what I mean?" Peter leaned into Libby and rested his head on her shoulder. "I get no privacy. Nothing is sacred."

"I don't mind." She turned and inhaled. Peter smelled like their warm, sleepy bodies and her faded perfume. Sleeping in Peter's arms felt like pure heaven, but now, as his mother pretended not to watch them, Libby sat up straighter and smoothed her rumpled clothes.

"Bring it right in." His mother held the door of the hotel suite open.

Two waiters wheeled in carts filled with food. As they set up a breakfast buffet on the table, the aroma of bacon, pancakes, and mini quiches filled her nose. On the road trip to Denver she only ate fast food, Cheetos, and red licorice.

"Lordy, look at all that food. Are we having a party?" DarLynn wandered into the living area wrapped in a fluffy robe embroidered with the hotel logo.

"Good morning, DarLynn, did you sleep well?" Peter's mother asked, sounding chipper.

"The bed sure was comfy, but I barely slept trying to stay awake and keep an eye on these two. Let's just say I'm not looking forward to all the late nights chaperoning my boys."

Libby's face warmed. "Oh my God," she said under her breath to Peter. Chaperoned? How humiliating. "You didn't need to stay up. We were just fine. Plus, Peter's eighteen. We're both adults now."

"Now, now, I'll hear nothing of it. He may be eighteen, but you're not. If your mother were here, do you think she'd leave you alone all night with a boy and a hotel full of beds?" DarLynn crossed her arms, a gesture Libby's mom often used when irritated.

Heat crept up her neck again. No doubt, her mom would have done the same as DarLynn. Peter squeezed her hand.

"By the way, something's wrong with that tub in there. It's all sparkly and pretty, but the darn jets are so strong, they kept shooting me from one side to the other. I'm surprised such a fancy-schmancy place would have a faulty tub."

Peter winked at Libby and grinned. Little tingles shot down to her toes.

"DarLynn, why don't you and I fix a plate and visit while the kids wake up and plan their day," Peter's mom said. "Plus, I can't wait to hear more about your darling boys. I have experience on how to handle three headstrong youngsters."

"What's that?" DarLynn asked. "Put 'em in a band?"

"Exactly."

While the women chatted like long-lost friends, Libby and Peter filled their plates. They huddled together at the granite counter and ate. She had never expected to see him again, and sitting so close was a fantasy come true. He seemed to agree as he picked that moment to kiss her. She knew their time together would go fast and parting wouldn't be easy.

They decided to spend the day hiking beautiful Granite Peak just outside of Denver. Roger found a trail off the beaten path, free from hordes of hikers. Thankfully, he stayed in the parking lot so Libby and Peter could spend the day alone.

It took a couple hours to hike to the top of what seemed like a mountain, but was probably just a bluff or foothill by Colorado standards. Surrounded by the scent of pine and a light breeze, the outside world fell away as if only they existed. Huge outcroppings of rocks, sprinkled with occasional brush and trees, covered the peak. They sprawled against a warm boulder and enjoyed a spectacular view of the nearby mountains. Libby lifted her water bottle, took a long drink, then passed it to Peter. He offered a bag of trail mix in return.

A strong August breeze cooled their warm skin. Libby leaned back and turned her head to Peter. He wore his baseball cap backward, presenting his gorgeous face. She could stare at him forever.

"What are you looking at?" His bright eyes seemed to smirk.

"You. I can't believe this is happening. I never dreamt I'd see you again."

"All this time apart, and you didn't even dream about me?" he teased.

"Stop it. You know that's not true." She took his hand and laced her fingers with his.

"I never stopped thinking about you." He kissed the top of her hand.

"Really?" She couldn't believe he cared so much. How could she be this lucky?

"Really," he said.

"So tell me about your dreams," Libby said.

"Now that I have you, there's not much left."

She snuggled closer. "You've accomplished so much, more than most people do in a lifetime. But you can't be done dreaming at eighteen. That would be tragic."

"Let's see, where do I begin?" He shifted to a more comfortable position, with Libby's back against his chest, his arms wrapped comfortably around her. "Our last album went platinum in a week and our upcoming tour sold out in minutes. That's all great, but I want to write the kind of music that lives on for decades. I'd like to move people with the power of my lyrics and music."

Libby lay against him. The sun beat down on their bodies as his breath tickled her neck like a feather.

"Then I'd like to take all the success I've enjoyed and do something really good with it. I'd like to help kids and sick people."

She listened to the low timbre of his voice, feeling it vibrate in his chest as she rested against him. He would do all these things. She knew he would.

"I'd also like to get my own place. You know, travel when I want to and not necessarily with my family. I love them, but it's time to grow up and live my life. At least as much as possible."

She contemplated all he said.

"And what about you?" He nipped the edge of her ear. "I've been blabbing away. Now that you're legally independent, what do you want to do with your life, besides go on tour and hang out with me 24/7?" He caressed her palm with his thumb.

She'd been plotting and planning for months, and it seemed everything clicked all at once. "First, I want to go to school and become a graphic artist. I've been drawing ever since my mom gave me my first box of crayons. It's the one thing I've always loved. I'd never make much money as a regular artist, but as a graphic artist I could always take care of myself."

Peter rested his chin in the nook of her neck. "I'll take care of you now."

She nestled closer. Reality began to seep into their perfect world. "That's sweet, but I've left my fate to others too many times, and it didn't work out, to say the least. I won't ever do that again. Now I need to take charge of my life."

"But I get to be in it, don't I?" he teased.

"Of course you do." She turned in his arms and reached up for a kiss. Peter set his lips upon hers. The touch of his kisses lit her on fire.

Content to be together and needing nothing more, they hung out at the top long enough for clouds to move in and shed a light sprinkle of rain. On their way back down the mountain, Peter told her about the preparations for their upcoming tour, appearances on the Video Music Awards, and *Saturday Night Live*. She told him about her preparations to start college in Boston this fall, and the heartbreak of her failed efforts to track down her dad. Now that she had her independence, she would keep her name public, so her dad could easily find her, should he be looking. No more hiding.

• • •

When they returned to the hotel, Peter needed an hour to shower and catch up on some band obligations. After that they would go to dinner.

DarLynn waited for her in their hotel suite. "You two have a good day?"

Libby bubbled with excitement like one of DarLynn's boys on his birthday. It was apparent how much DarLynn wanted Libby to find happiness. "We did, thanks. I can't believe we're actually here. I can never thank you enough."

"Aw, it's been my pleasure. I haven't had this much fun since, well, since never. I got to see a Jamieson concert, make friends with Peter's momma, and stay in this swanky hotel. The boys will never believe all our stories. Look at all the amazing stuff Karen brought over for the boys, and it's all autographed."

Libby looked through the pile of Jamieson T-shirts, hats, and CDs. The boys would love the gifts.

"Oh, and Peter's dad had the truck fixed, so we can head back anytime."

Libby's head snapped up. She knew they needed to leave soon, but still, the announcement caught her off guard. She didn't want to face reality yet. She needed a little longer.

"And none too soon," DarLynn continued. "I called home today and all hell is breakin' loose. The motel over in Greenville had a fire, and now the Twilight is plum overflowing. The baby's got the flu, so Bea's been cleaning up hurl all day. Jimmy's momma can't handle stress too well, and it sounds like she's hitting the bottle again. She's better as a glittery ornament than as a grown-up getting her fingernails dirty. Oh, and Bea said Penny's short another waitress. Apparently, Vera ran off with her boyfriend the morning we left. Can you imagine so much happening in just a coupla days?"

Libby pictured poor Penny trying to keep her business running when she was short two waitresses. The woman must be exhausted. And Robby sick, the little sweetheart. The realities of life slapped her cold across the face; it was time for her fantasy trip to end and go back.

"When do you want to leave?" Libby asked, willing to do whatever necessary. She and Peter hadn't figured out the future yet. She didn't want to leave him, but knew she couldn't stay, either.

"Oh, honey, we can wait till tomorrow. I don't want to spoil your reunion with that hottie boy of yours. Darn, you didn't tell me he could melt chocolate with those smoking good looks. You're the luckiest girl I know."

Libby smiled at her remarks. Lucky, yes, despite all the loss and pain in her past. Just then, Peter let himself into the suite. His eyes glittered with excitement.

"Hi, DarLynn," he greeted her.

"Hi there yourself." DarLynn smiled coyly.

He crossed the room to Libby. "I talked to my mom and dad, and we've got it all worked out."

"What are you talking about?" she asked.

"Us. Our plans."

"Oh."

"There's good news and bad news." He looked like a little kid with a big secret.

"Okay, tell me." She fought back her laugh.

"First, the good news." He paused for effect. "You're coming on tour with me. It starts in early September, but you can stay with us. You'll get to travel the country. We have a second bus now, so we won't have to be hassled by my family all the time. Of course, my parents insisted that one of them or Roger be around, but we'll be together."

She'd never seen him so happy, and she loved it, but had he forgotten about her starting school?

"Now the bad news. I have to leave tonight. I can't believe this is happening, but the first release from our new album is due to hit in a few days along with the music video. There was some sort of mix-up at the editing company and a full minute of tape is corrupted." He pushed his hands through his hair. "Something about a system failure and inadequate off-site backup systems. Anyway, we have to re-film the missing scenes. It's an outdoor shoot at the Pike Place fishermen's market in Seattle."

"Okay." She tried to follow his confusing explanation.

"The problem is, a storm is coming in and the only window of time to get the shooting done is tomorrow, so Adam, Garrett, and I have to fly out tonight. I'm so sorry.

But I can be back tomorrow night or the next day for sure. Crud, that's not true. The day after, we have rehearsals for the Video Music Awards, but you could still fly out and join me. It'll be a lot of industry stuff, but at least we'll be together part of the time."

Something inside Libby clicked, as if suddenly she could see the future clearly and all the problems and pitfalls, all the realities of each of their lives. She glanced at DarLynn, who pretended to occupy herself with the television remote. "Peter, come with me."

Libby took him by the hand and led him out on the balcony for privacy. Once she closed the patio doors, they stood at the railing overlooking the beautiful skyline of downtown Denver.

"Are you okay?" Concern etched his face.

"I'm fine." She nodded with a heavy heart and took a deep breath for courage and hoped she handled this right. "I love you. You do know that, don't you?"

"Yeah, I know." He squeezed her hand and smiled at her.

"It's great that you're making all these plans for us, but have you forgotten that I'm starting school in a few weeks?" As much as she'd love to follow him and share his rock-star life, she wanted—no, needed—more than anything to go to school for herself, her future.

"Oh. Well, yeah, I guess I kind of did. I'm just so happy to have you back. I don't want to miss a second of being together." He grinned, looking more adorable than ever.

"I know. But from what you just said, it sounds like it's going to be hard to spend any time together. And I have to leave in the morning to get back to my jobs in Pebble Creek. People are counting on me."

His face fell.

"Peter. When I met you, my life was so miserable, and you saved me from the darkest depths and led me back to happiness. And after that, when everything fell apart and I thought you didn't want to see me again, you still gave me strength. The happiness you gave me translated into determination to stop getting pushed around. You gave me the courage and power to walk out of that group home and start making my own decisions. I could never have done that without you."

Peter looked worried. His brows turned down and his jaw tightened.

"What are you doing?" he asked, his voice leery.

Libby didn't know how to say this. She'd love to share his crazy rock-star life, but deep down knew she couldn't. "I'm trying to explain this to you. You need to know how profoundly you have affected my life."

"Libby, please don't." He shifted on his feet.

"If there is one thing I've learned this past year, it's that I have to be in charge of my life. No one else. I want to go to college and get a degree. I really do. I can't go on tour with you and still do that. I have to be able to take care of myself for the rest of my life. I can't leave that to someone else again."

"Stop talking like this." Peter tried to turn away. She pulled him back.

"And as much as I'd love to be with you, I would only hold you back. You are needed so many places all the time. You have music to write, interviews to tape, and concerts to perform. We'd barely ever see each other anyway."

Libby knew she was breaking his heart. Heck, she was breaking her own.

Peter searched her eyes and seemed to make a decision. "Change of plans. Come with me tonight. I will make this work. I promise you. I'll figure this out so we can be together. Every second I'm not working, I'm with you." He held her hands and looked into her eyes with such love and hope.

She smiled sadly.

Peter shoved a hand through his hair. "God, Libby, please don't leave me now. You don't need your job anymore. Let me take care of you for once. I have plenty of money."

"This isn't about money. There are a handful of people back in Pebble Creek who moved heaven and earth to help me get here. And now they need me to help them. I need to go back with DarLynn."

Peter shook his head, his eyes glassy with pain.

She squeezed his hand and spoke softly. "You need to go catch your plane and take care of the video."

"I'll quit the band."

"No, you won't. You are the most gifted person I've ever known. You're too smart to walk away from your music." She reached up and smoothed his golden hair.

"We can do this. Give it a chance."

"I don't see how? You can't give up performing and I can't skip out on school. You're from out west and I'll be living on the East Coast. I'm not saying we can't see each other and stay connected, but I just don't think anything more is going to work right now."

Peter released her, rested his arms on the balcony rail, and stared into the distance.

She joined him. "These past twenty-four hours have been an amazing dream come true. But it's time to get back to our lives. I've got only a few weeks to wrap up things in Georgia before I leave for school.

"I will always love you and now that we've found each other, I want to always remain friends, but to try to hold a relationship together is too much. When I'm in school, I can't take off for days at a time. I'd never succeed. And you wouldn't succeed trying to constantly get away to be with me. Am I making sense?"

"I'm not going to answer that," he said stubbornly.

She smiled. He got it. He just didn't want to admit it.

He took her hand and pulled her to him, burying his face in her hair. "Damn it, Libby. I can't let you go," he murmured in her ear. "I can't do it." His voice broke with emotion.

She tried not to cry. As much as she wanted to, she couldn't give in, this was too important. "You need to go one direction, and I need to go another."

"I don't like it."

"I don't, either," she said and meant it. But she'd learned that sometimes hard decisions were the only way to make it in life. "But we'll take the love with us. No one can ever take that away."

A knock on the patio door interrupted them. Adam peered out. They released each other. Peter turned away from the door, hiding the anguish on his face. Libby waved Adam over to join them.

"Hey, Adam," she said, her sadness clear.

"Hey." He looked worried as he took in their tortured expressions. "Sorry to interrupt but, Peter, we gotta go."

Poor Adam looked miserable knowing she and Peter would be separated again.

"I'll be there in a sec," Peter said, not facing him.

Adam quietly left them alone, each in their private pain. Libby fought to keep her composure, but each moment became more heartbreaking.

Peter turned to her abruptly. "I won't let you do this."

"It'll never work. This will be better in the long run," she said, breaking her own heart.

"Stop." He put his finger on her lips, then leaned forward and replaced them with his lips. His kiss was gentle and soft as if healing a wound. Then he became more urgent as if sending her a message, a promise of something more to come. She clung to him, wanting to prolong their time together. Tears rolled from her eyes. Peter kissed them away. She fought to hold her emotions in.

"I want you to call me. Promise?" His eyes were dark and sad in the early evening dusk, as if holding up the weight of the world. When she didn't answer, he gave her a little shake. "Promise."

She nodded, but knew she wouldn't. It would be easier to let him go this way. He didn't need her holding him back.

They turned at the sound of Roger opening the patio door. "It's time," he said, avoiding eye contact, then departed discreetly, but left the door open. Peter's parents and brothers waited inside the suite next to a somber-looking DarLynn.

Libby flung herself into Peter's arms and hugged him tight, wanting to remember everything about him. "I love you," she whispered, then released him and turned back to the skyline. "Now go, before I embarrass myself in front of your family."

"This isn't over," he murmured in her ear.

She stood for long minutes, gulping back her grief, watching the lights of the city pop on as the sun sank behind a mountain in the distance. The sunset created a spectacular display of colors on the evening sky. When she turned around, the hotel suite was empty, except for DarLynn packing Libby's bag.

27

Two weeks had passed since she said good-bye to Peter. She missed him so much, but was determined to let him move on and live his life without trying to take care of her. Parting again felt like picking at an old wound. The only good part was that this time it was on her terms, and she and Peter had had the chance to say good-bye. She tried to focus on the next two weeks. She needed to wrap up her life in Pebble Creek and get ready to start school. She carried dirty dishes past Penny, who kept peeking out the window.

"What are you looking at?" Libby glanced out and saw nothing out of the ordinary.

"Oh, nothing, just watching traffic." She wore a crooked smile on her face.

Libby left Penny to her spying and returned dirty coffee cups to the dish cart. "What's got you in such a fine mood?" she asked as she grabbed two clean glasses.

Penny appeared at her side, grinning like a crazy woman.

"Everything okay?" Libby eyed her suspiciously as she filled a glass with orange soda.

"I'm really gonna miss you," she said, twisting a dish towel. Her boss was acting like a grandma gone kooky.

"What are you talking about?" Libby asked.

A loud rumbling sounded outside the building. The front window rattled.

"What is that?" Libby glanced up. Penny tried to block her view.

A familiar silver tour bus pulled up in front of the café. She immediately forgot the soda and looked to Penny in question. Her friend rewarded her with a warm and loving smile, but said nothing.

Libby staggered to the window in a trance. She'd recognize that bus anywhere. The massive vehicle filled the street, causing passersby to stop and stare. Peter was here! In Pebble Creek. Her stomach flipped in anticipation of seeing him again.

The tour bus door opened. Libby held her breath. The amazing and gorgeous Peter Jamieson appeared on the steps and hopped off. He held something small in his hand. When he saw her in the window, a sexy smile crossed his face. She bit her lower lip to hold back squeals of euphoria.

"That is one good-looking boy," Penny said from Libby's side.

She couldn't agree more. "Why is he here?"

"Get out there and find out." Penny nudged her toward the door.

Libby wiped her hands on her apron and walked outside. She hoped the onlookers couldn't see how much she wanted to run and leap into his arms. Her eyes drifted to his and locked. She couldn't look away if her life depended on it.

"What is going on? Peter, why are you here?" Not that he needed a reason. She knew now she'd been wrong to suggest they live apart.

He flashed his sexy eyes. "First, here's a new phone. I hope you use it often." He smiled slow and easy.

She accepted the new phone, her lifeline to Peter back and fully powered.

"After talking to DarLynn and your friends here, we decided you've been working too hard and need a vacation," Peter said.

She looked behind her to find DarLynn, Penny, and Jerrold beaming.

Peter continued. "So I've cleared my schedule. You and I are taking a road trip." He gestured and grinned toward the bus.

"But I still have two weeks left to work." She turned to Penny for explanation. She desperately wanted to go with Peter, but wouldn't leave Penny in a lurch.

"Don't you worry about a thing." Penny stepped forward

and unpinned Libby's name tag. "Your boyfriend here gave me notice two weeks ago that you needed to quit early for this trip."

"Peter, is that true?" She turned to face him, giddy that Penny referred to him as her boyfriend.

"I hope you don't mind. I didn't think you'd go without a team effort to kick you out of town."

The kindness in his eyes warmed her like a late summer sun. Words escaped her. Penny untied Libby's apron strings and slid the garment from her hips.

"You always said you wanted to travel the country, so we're going to see what we can fit in before you start college."

"Peter, why are you doing all this? Are you crazy?"

He grinned. "Yup, pretty much. There is no way I'm letting you go this easy. We have time to make up. Oh yeah, I forgot to mention that I bought a condo in Boston. Did you know that forty percent of the cities we tour are within five hours of Boston? Turns out you picked a perfect place to go to school."

Her mind was awhirl. With him based in Boston, they would have plenty of time to spend together without ruining his career or keeping her from school.

"I don't know what to say." It was difficult to take it all in.

"Listen," he said gently, and stepped closer. "No one can predict the future, but right now you're the most important thing to me. I will regret it for the rest of my life if we don't give this a chance."

He took her hands in his and caressed her scarred palms. "You say the word and I'll go away. It's up to you."

She looked in his beautiful eyes; she saw love and hope.

"When do we leave?"

Acknowledgments

Writing a novel starts with the bud of an idea, something deep down that wants to be heard or a question of "what if?" So without naming him, I want to acknowledge the sweet kid who inspired this story. Too many kids are forced to deal with heartache, and his story touched my soul.

Special thanks go out to my critique partners, beta readers, and contributors: Linda Schmalz, Deb Barkelar, Liz Reinhardt, Margo Zimmerman, Abbi Glines, Mary Kay Adams, Claire Courchane, and Kristi Tyler.

Thank you to the many people who assisted with research, including Emily Becker, Colleen Hoover, and Ellen Smith. A special bow of gratitude to James Dylan, the lead singer of Jason Bonham's Led Zeppelin Experience. It's been a blast learning about your world. You rock!

And to Ed, Kristi, and Kevin, none of this would mean anything without you. You listen to my crazy ideas and always nod and smile, even though deep down you think I'm nuts. You're right, but it's nice that you pretend I'm not.

Thank you to my agent, Jane Dystel, for your confidence and commitment. Your kindness makes me miss my mom.

Without a corporate office to report to each day, the job of a writer can be lonely. So to my fabulous writer buds, the girls of FP, you crazies are my people, my coworkers, and the friends I sneak online to chat with every day. You talk me off the cliff, you lift me up, and you make me laugh. Pagina sparklers for all!

Finally, to Rosemary Brosnan, editorial director at HarperCollins Children's Books, thank you for sending the best Facebook message a girl could ever dream of.